ROANOKE
ISLAND

ATL

OC

ENGLAND

ROUTE OF THE
LION

PLYMOUTH

TIC

N

N

E

W

S

EDWARD CORTESE

Lost
Colony

Lost Colony

The Mystery of Roanoke Island

By JEAN BOTHWELL

Illustrated by Edward F. Cortese

HOLT, RINEHART AND WINSTON

New York • Chicago • San Francisco

$$\frac{N.C.}{J}$$

C. 3

For Margaret Ayer
In Appreciation

The Story of Roanoke

AFTER three hundred years the scent is cold, yet the story of the Lost Colony of Roanoke has remained one of the foremost topics of historical speculation among English-speaking people. How a group of over one hundred persons—men, women and children—could vanish, leaving only one slight clue to their destination or intention, has fascinated historians, worried scientists, and eluded solution.

Many theories have been advanced as to what might have happened, some of them plausible, one or two possible. One of these possibilities, that they were induced to move because of fear of unfriendly Indians and lack of supplies, and intermarried with the friendly tribe which had taken them in, has good support.

On the mainland today, in North Carolina, there are English names among the people of mixed Indian and white blood which were on the original roster of the Roanoke Colony and their speech contains many words now obsolete in the English language. While it is true that there were other English colonists who came in later, and some of the original Jamestown colony migrated to the Carolinas, there is sufficient oral history to indicate that some of them may stem from the original Roanoke Colony.

One historian believes that when Governor White returned to the White-Dare Colony, he so vaguely remembered where they were that he went to the wrong island. Afraid of the captain and crew, he dared not admit his mistake and furthered the idea that the colony was lost, with only the word *Croatan* to explain their absence.

Whether or not Governor White was on the wrong island and whether or not the single word *Croatan* had been put on the tree by his own or other colonists, he was never able to follow up the search and see if he had been mistaken in his identification, or whether they really had gone to Croatan Island, as seemed possible.

In 1937, to commemorate the three hundred and fiftieth anniversary of the birth of Virginia Dare, the Roanoke Island Historical Association commissioned and produced a play called *The Lost Colony,* which was given at the site of old Fort Raleigh, on Roanoke Island. The denouement, according to the playwright, Paul Green, is migration to the mainland because the colonists had sighted a Spanish ship. Geographically, this couldn't have happened, as the location of the colony would prevent any such warning.

One liberty has been taken with history. There were three ships which left Plymouth, *The Lion,* a pinnace and the flyboat. The last was left at some spot in the Bay of Portugal. There were 150 householders signed up and the list as preserved counts about 117, which means that the rest were probably in the flyboat. Two ships arrived at Roanoke. But after the flyboat was lost, for the sake of clarity, no mention was made of a second ship.

CECILE MATSCHAT, *Editor*
CARL CARMER, *Consulting Editor*

CONTENTS

CHAPTER 1

The Inn by the Sea

THOMAS HUMPHREY HALL plodded wearily along the road. He had been walking from Gilling in Yorkshire toward the English coast and he meant to sail on *The Lion* from Plymouth harbor, if he could get there in time. He set his jaw and muttered as he went. There must be no ifs. He would sail.

He lifted his face. Rain. There had been clouds that May morning of 1587, and now, at evening, on his fifth day of walking, they were fulfilling their promise. He must find shelter, quickly. Getting wet and having a fever would not help his

1

plans. He set his lips more firmly. Even the weather must not make any difference. He would sail.

It was a lonely bit of road he was on, not even a farmhouse in sight, and the hedgerows were thin. No shelter under them. So far he had avoided the country inns which lay along his route. Such public places would be the first thought of a pursuer, an angry uncle, say, asking for a runaway boy. He looked about him again, shielding his eyes from the rain with a hand to his forehead.

He saw smoke, then, a low-lying ribbon of it, against a field ahead. One might almost mistake it for mist, rolling low on the ground. But he was sure it was smoke, which meant people, and though it was a risk, he stumbled forward hopefully.

The road led downward and around the field which was really the top of a little hill. Against it, in a small hollow, was an inn, a quiet place, almost too quiet, as if not caring to advertise itself. It had a sign, but the name was too faded to read. A few sad-looking pack ponies stood in the stable yard.

Even if it did look forlorn, the boy decided he could find food and a dry place out of the wet, so he crossed the cobbles and entered. Three men were there in the public room around a table, talking in low voices. The close air was heavy with the smell of cooking and the odor of the men's damp clothing. But the warmth from the hearth fire was good after the rain, and Humphrey stood shaking himself like a happy dog getting rid of excess moisture.

A girl, who seemed for all her plumpness and matronly cap little older than himself, and he had been fourteen last Michaelmas Day, appeared behind the inn desk, and asked what he wanted.

"Supper and a bed," said Humphrey.

The girl looked him over, calculatingly, from head to toe.

Humphrey flushed. "I can pay," he said.

"Show me your siller," said the girl.

Humphrey felt in the inner pocket of his jacket and produced one of his gold florins, saved from birthdays past. There had been no need for spending at Gilling.

The girl's face changed, and she looked him over again, a long minute, before she took out a key and said, "Come!"

She led him through the big room to the stairway, and he followed close at her heels, conscious of his soiled clothes, of the silence at the table and the eyes of the men boring into his back.

Upstairs and inside a somewhat shabby chamber, the girl stood with her back to the door and faced Humphrey, looking him over for a third time, head to toe, seeing the riding clothes he wore, his high soft leather boots and hatless head.

"What's the meaning o' it, young master? Don't ye know where ye are? What brings ye? Flashing out yer gold! Are ye clean daft?"

"I'm . . . I'm . . . I've been walking, and I'm hungry. I want only to sup and sleep and be on my way when the rain stops."

"And yer way?"

"Lies along the road to Plymouth . . ."

Too late, Humphrey realized what he had said. His hand flew to his lips in dismay.

The girl laughed. "I believe ye, now. There's boats at Plymouth, and for all ye're not wearin' sailor's gear . . ." She nodded, knowingly, and bustled over to the fireplace to light the ready-laid kindling.

"You trust Phoebe and I'll set ye on the road. Ye've an honest face. Too honest. Have ye no idea where ye are? Tell me true!"

Humphrey shook his head, bewildered by the repeated question, and the girl laughed again.

"Bide here," she said, "an' I'll bring ye some hot water and a bite. Wherever home is they'd never let ye sup without washin' that face."

While he waited for his supper, Humphrey crossed to the window and stood looking out. The room was just above the entrance to the inn and the sign hung below him. There was nothing to see but the bit of road along which he had come round the hill, but far away he could hear a dull booming, a bang and a crash, that went on and on. The ocean! He was close to it. He had made good time, indeed. Tomorrow he would be in Plymouth. He would sail.

Nearer than the sea another sound could be heard in the wind. It was the creaking of the board which held the faded name of the house. It came in a regular beat, faint, then louder, and a phrase in Humphrey's mind began to keep time to it. "You can do it. You can do it," over and over again.

That was what Eleanor Dare had said, back there in York, those many weeks ago, when plans for Sir Walter Raleigh's colony in the New World were first talked about. Her father, John White, was to be its governor. Her husband, Ananias Dare, was a Raleigh Patentee, to help in all colony business.

Much of the talking had been done by the fire in the dining room of the Dare house at Gilling, and Humphrey forgot his hunger and his weariness as that picture rose in his mind. He had held wool for Eleanor to wind, or sat with idle hands as she sewed on small jackets for the child she would bear in the coming summer, her first.

He should have been at lessons, they both knew, but what did lessons matter if he could slip away and go on the same ship with Eleanor and Ananias? When he said, longingly, "I wish I could go," she laid her knitting aside and looked him in the eye.

"You can, Humphrey. You can do it," she said firmly.

Eleanor herself had not wanted to make the voyage. " 'Nias reminds me that English women must be brave. The stories of the New World do sound exciting. But there is never any mention of hearths and homes, Humphrey, the things women care about. Have you noticed how much they talk of gold and savages?"

"The gold will not matter if there are no shops," said Humphrey. "The savages may try to kill us, but not without a fine fight, first. It will be exciting, Eleanor. That is part of why I want to go."

The other part Eleanor had known already.
There was his loneliness in the house across the
great park from the Dares since his mother had
died. There was his Uncle Jeremy's decision to
send him almost immediately to London to become a courtier. There was his own desire to remain in the country and in time manage his own
lands. He could do that, he knew. Old Robin,
their head farmer, had said so more than once.

Land! There were heaps of it in the New
World, they said, free for the settling. He remembered now that he had reminded Eleanor,
"Perhaps the ground in the New World will be
good for crops, too, as well as gold. I might have
another manor of my own, there."

Eleanor had laid the tips of her fingers against
his cheek. "I know, Humphrey. You shall come
with us, if I can help. I wish there were some way
to get you to Plymouth. I am sorry you must
manage that alone. But you can do it."

Now here he was, standing by a window near
another fire, almost at the end of his walk, listening to those words again, though they were only
in his mind.

He thought he heard the room door open, but
when he turned he saw that it was closed as
Phoebe had left it. Then, in the dim light of the

fire and the candle, he saw a tall crack beside the hearth, slowly growing wider, and the soft rattle of a dish lid. His supper was arriving in an odd fashion. One would not know there was any other door to this room. When he came in, the paneling had been flush with the fireplace.

Phoebe stepped softly down from the last stair tread and laid a finger to her lip before she spread the supper on a small table. There was no hot water for washing.

"Sit down, young master. Ye haven't much time. They're after ye. I heard the talk. Yer gold was too much for 'em. Didn't ye know it would be smugglers in this place, so close to the sea? I tried to hint ye, but ye wouldna take it."

Humphrey looked at her, not fully comprehending, and she pushed him down into a chair, and offered him the serving dishes, one by one.

It was not easy to eat. Humphrey's throat felt tight and his heart thumped beneath his dusty, stained jacket. If anything happened, if they held him to get more gold, he would miss the ship. He looked up at Phoebe.

"It's very good, but I can't eat any more."

"Then take it with ye," she said. "Come. Make ready. Take off yer boots for a start."

He obeyed while Phoebe rolled bread and

meat in the coarse linen cloth from the table. She
picked up the bundle, and he carried his boots
and followed her into the narrow stairway. She
pulled the panel door tight shut behind them,
and he heard a clicking sound. Then they
climbed in complete darkness. At the top Phoebe
reached for Humphrey's hand.

"We're in the attics," she whispered, "and ye'll
have to stoop. I don't want ye on my hands with
a cracked head."

Humphrey's sore muscles protested every step
he took in that crouching fashion, and he was
glad when they came to another, similarly narrow stair, which wound away down in the same

strange dark. Phoebe took it sidewise with a sure step, her hand reached back to touch Humphrey's and guide him. At the foot she said, "Hist!" and opened the door a hair's crack.

"Put on yer boots," she whispered, "so's ye can run, if ye must."

When she was sure of safety they came out into the inn kitchen. It was a warm place and Humphrey would have liked staying in it, if only a little while, to get warm. But Phoebe had no such idea.

"Now then, young master," she said, "Phoebe'll set ye on the road as promised."

"But they will punish you," Humphrey protested.

She tossed her head. "It's my father's inn. He's away just now. Come now! I slipped yer bolt inside, above, so they'll think ye still there. Here!"

She thrust the packet of food at him and caught up a long black mantle from the settle in the kitchen. She blew out the candle and opened the back door of the inn. Above the sound of the rain there was laughter from the public room.

"Don't talk now," said Phoebe.

She led the way again, across the cobbles of the yard and around to the front of the building.

Humphrey looked up. There was a faint glow in
the window above the sign. It was the candle left
burning there and the light the fire might give.
If those ruffians waited for it to die out, he could
be safe away. Phoebe was smart!

The rain was pelting down. When they were
out in the road, Phoebe held the great loose cape
wide and threw an end over Humphrey's head,
completely sheltering him from the wet. It was
awkward walking and in spite of his gratitude
Humphrey felt annoyance deep inside him when
he smelled the oil in Phoebe's heavy hair. In the

next minute he felt shame. She was helping him on his road to the New World. In that moment he felt he could do anything to make the coast and the ship.

They walked thus perhaps a mile and Humphrey's heart had resumed its even beat again when Phoebe spoke. She lifted the cape as she did so.

"Ye'll be all right now, young master. Hereabouts is a good shelter for ye for the rest of the night. Nobody knows it but me."

Phoebe slipped the cape away completely then

and the crash of waves was close. They had reached the coast. In the lee of a great boulder, above the tide mark, Phoebe pointed out a small dry hollow, into which Humphrey crawled gratefully. He could not stand up in it, but that did not matter.

He offered the change from the gold piece with which he had paid his charge earlier in the evening, but Phoebe refused it.

"Nay," she said, "ye'll need it before ye get to the New World maybe. Ye paid enough. I am sorry about the hot water but I had to hurry after I heard the plan to waylay ye in yer bed. Sleep now. They won't find ye here and it won't be long until morning."

Phoebe turned away and then Humphrey heard her step again and she spoke anxiously, "Young master, do be careful. Ye're too trustin'. Now, good luck go wi' all yer journeys."

At sunrise Humphrey scrambled out of his snug resting place and climbed to the top of the great boulder, where he ate a small portion of the bread and meat Phoebe had given him. He wrapped the remaining food in a crumpled silk kerchief from his pocket, the better for carrying. If the rest of the country between him and Plymouth was as barren as that around the inn, he must save every crumb. He slept again, a little, and when he waked, he saw, peeking out cautiously, that he would not be alone on this road.

Carts were going by. Some of them were piled with household goods. That was odd. Where would people be moving to, along a stormy coast road? The stuff wouldn't be smugglers', not out in the open this way.

All the carts were going in the same direction, the one he himself was traveling. Why might they not be carrying colonists' goods, heading as he was for the good ship *Lion* and thence to the New World?

CHAPTER 2

Off Plymouth Hoe

I T was early afternoon by the time Humphrey entered the town of Plymouth and made his way, unnoticed, to the Hoe, a hill overlooking the harbor. Crowds of townspeople had gathered there to watch the business going on along the quay. More were arriving.

"My brother is going," Humphrey heard a man say. "Viccars is the name."

"And my cousin, Miss Lawrence," said another. "She travels with the Harvies. They haven't arrived yet." He looked about, anxiously.

16

"Plenty of time," said the first, sounding important. "The captain plans to go out with the tide early tomorrow morning."

Humphrey looked around carefully. No one had eyes for a lone, dirty boy who had followed country carts in along the coast road that morning. The noise coming up from the quay sounded to him like a Nottingham fair. He went down into it slowly, noting everything. Travelers and tradesmen had gathered around the stacks of stores and household goods there, and the sailors were having a hard time to push a way through and load the stuff into the hold of the ship.

A cow was led in at a door in the waist, her calf following docilely. Other cows, already aboard, greeted them, bawling loudly. Geese honked and hissed in a stout pen sent in after the cow. Some pieces of household furniture, chests and dressers and high-backed, carved chairs, followed the livestock. There was one hooded cradle. Humphrey recognized that piece. Eleanor Dare herself had been rocked in it when she was a babe.

He saw landing stairs, lashed securely to the side of the ship, leading up from the quay. It might be a good idea to find a place aboard to hide until sailing time. He began to climb a little breathlessly. At the top he had another heart-stopping moment, worse than the one the night before when Phoebe had told him of his danger. An officer, with arms behind his back and feet spread wide apart, barred his way.

"Who are you? What's your name?" the officer asked.

"Thomas Humphrey." He felt as if he were shouting it. He had not been obliged to answer that question since he had left Gilling.

The officer looked at his paper and back at Humphrey. "The name of Thomas Humphrey is written here among the single men. A boy, traveling alone, it would seem, turns up to claim it. How did they make such a mistake?"

The sailor looked the new arrival over, head to toe, and Humphrey returned the look, eye to eye.

The seaman saw that this Thomas Humphrey had come a long way. He wore no hat. There was dust in his eyebrows and lashes. His nostrils and mouth had the drawn look of complete weariness. His tight jacket was well cut, but it and his high soft boots were dusty, too, and he smelled of the stable. Under one arm he hugged a small knobby bundle wrapped in a grease-spotted silk kerchief.

The boy saw a hard, tightly pressed mouth,

and a calculating look in the keen eye appraising him. "How old are you?"

"Fourteen."

The officer wrote it down on the list, opposite the name.

"I am strong. I can work. As much as a man does," Humphrey added.

"They always can, boys like you who run away to sea," said the seaman. "How you got yourself on this list is never-no-matter now. But you are not going to stay on it. Don't you know how plain it is that you are a runaway?"

Humphrey's shoulders squared. The look on his tired face changed to alert fear. "But, Sir, I am not alone. Not exactly. 'Tis true I have arrived alone, but I . . . I know the Dares. We were neighbors . . . I am of their party."

"Ho-ho! So it is Yorkshire I smell. You have come far, young fellow."

"How can you know?"

The officer grinned. 'Tis well-known that the Dares are of York. Well . . ." he hesitated. "You look honest. You do mean to sail? You could be planning to right-about and slip ashore when no one is looking. That would be a new dodge to lose oneself, and you look sharp enough for it. Friend of the Dares or not, I still think you are a runaway."

"Nay, Sir, I sail, if . . ." Humphrey bit his lip. There must be no ifs. He looked toward the quay apprehensively.

The sailor saw the look. "So you do mean to sail!" he said. "Well, get along with you. I'm busy. Don't let me see you again before dark. I know who has come aboard and who has not."

He winked broadly, and reached a large hand to pat Humphrey's shoulder, and dust flew out from it in a little cloud. He laughed heartily and the boy smiled a bit uncertainly. It was difficult to do, somehow. There had been nothing but anxiety and fear along his road to this moment.

"Find yourself a corner to hide in," said the man. "You will sail. As you say, I think you may be useful, too, mighty useful."

He did not say in what way, and Humphrey did not wait to ask. He let his taut chest expand and gulped in gratefully a long breath of the salt air. How good the movement felt! He was aboard! Only a few more hours to wait!

He had never been on a ship before and was not sure how to make his search for a good place to see and be himself unnoticed. Busy sailors were all about, but no one stopped him when he went toward the stern of the ship and down an open-railed stair, to the well deck. He crossed it and went up again on the other side to the afterdeck. There, on the high poop, he found what he was looking for, a small space between the ship's railing and the high skylight coaming of the poop cabin. He could see the stir on the quay and passengers coming and going, and no one paid him any attention. He settled down crosslegged on the deck. He had nothing to do now but wait.

There were several things he had to wait for. The most important, of course, was the arrival of

the Dares and Governor White. Then, until the
ship sailed, he must be alert for fear Uncle Jeremy might trace him. If he did not, there was
still the anxiety as to what might happen when it
was learned that Thomas Humphrey was not a
grown man but a boy of fourteen.

Humphrey sat and thought of all these things
while his eyes followed the activity along shore.
He was sure now that he should have changed his
name to an entirely different one. But Eleanor
had insisted that shortening it in his letter of ap-
plication to Sir Walter would be quite enough.

Her only worry had been his getting to the
coast. She had promised to bring his clothes so
that he would not have that problem, but she
had firmly refused from the first to include his
hound, Tobey. The dog was too old for such exertion and including him would be too difficult.
For one thing, 'Nias would certainly have to be
told, and they must not do that, not if Humphrey
wished to sail.

Humphrey himself had had doubts that he
would escape from Uncle Jeremy, and a boy
traveling with a dog on country roads would be
more remarkable than one alone. He had to admit Eleanor's wisdom and give up the idea,
though it had made him almost sick when the

time came to slip away and leave old Tobey tied
and begging to come.

As for the letter, he had meant Sir Walter to
think him a single man, young and with no ties,
interested in the new venture, but without funds
to put in it, so he had omitted his exact age. If
there had been any inquiry from London, it had
come after he had left home. The chance of that
inquiry had been his greatest mistake in not
changing his name completely. He saw that now.
Uncle Jeremy, who was also his guardian, would
have no trouble in tracing him to *The Lion*. He
would not be fooled by two-thirds of a name.

Uncle Jeremy could be a powerful enemy.
The White family already had some. That was
why Eleanor had been afraid to tell Ananias of
their plans, for fear he would forbid them. It
was in the agreement with Sir Walter that no one
was obliged to stay in the New World if they did
not like the place. They might return to England some day, and Ananias could argue that they
must not make trouble with a neighbor. So Eleanor could not let Humphrey travel with her in
her comfortable, low-swung coach down through
the pleasant spring country to London and
thence to Plymouth. Ananias must not know
until it was too late for him to do anything.

All the way from Yorkshire uneasiness had walked and slept with Humphrey. Now it was a heavier burden because of the ship's officer with the list. Why had the man decided so suddenly to protect him?

Well, there was only one more night to worry about anything and then, if nothing happened by the time the tide flowed out the next morning, he would be free, his own man for the rest of his life. One did not need money in the New World. One found gold there, on the ground, so it was said. Let Uncle Jeremy keep what he was leaving behind him in England. If he sailed!

Humphrey shifted his position. He had sat still too long and one foot was numb. It would be good to lie down somewhere and let his whole body sleep. But he must keep watch until Eleanor should arrive.

More people had come aboard now and they began to crowd the railing, hiding the quay, so Humphrey ventured away from his shelter and stood among them, looking overside. Smooth, polished wood felt hot under his hand in the May sun.

In spite of his interest in what he was seeing, Humphrey fell to worrying again. What if something had happened to Eleanor's coach on the

OFF PLYMOUTH HOE
5

road? She was to meet Ananias in London. He
had gone ahead for a Patentees' meeting and
afterward he planned to present Eleanor to the
Queen. If Eleanor had fallen ill and there was
a delay, would the captain wait for them? If he
did, as he surely would, then Humphrey's hope
of going would shrink. There would also be still
another night to be anxious, if not more. There
would be more time for his uncle to follow on to
Plymouth.

At a shout from the shore Humphrey jumped,
startled out of his anxiety. A post coach was being
driven directly onto the quay, and the crowd was
parting before it. People began cheering when
Governor White appeared. Ananias Dare followed him and turned to help Eleanor down.
The Widow Pierce stepped forward then and
swept Mistress Dare a deep curtsy. Humphrey
had not noticed her until now and he wanted to
laugh. Jane Pierce was the midwife from Gilling
and at home the curtsy might not have been so
deep. Here the Widow had an audience. It was
good that she had come. Eleanor had at last said
she would not, if Jane were not persuaded, too.

The party from the coach began slowly to as-
cend the landing stairs. The women's full, long
skirts and traveling mantles were a hindrance.

Behind them were two strange-looking people, the like of which Humphrey had never seen. These must be the savages he had heard about, the copper-colored men from the forests of the New World. They were dressed in soft skins, even to the shoes on their feet and their straight hair looked blacker for the bright feather each wore, thrust in low at the neck.

The red men stalked solemnly behind Governor White's party and followed them into the captain's cabin when they reached the deck. Humphrey longed to rush forward and speak to

Eleanor, to let her know that he, too, had arrived safely. But before he could decide on the wisdom of such a public greeting, the door was shut.

It was almost sunset. Humphrey turned toward his shelter again. The remaining food in his bundle would be enough for tonight. He had decided to sleep out under the stars. He would not then be easily found in that company of over a hundred souls if his uncle should come.

The stars came out and the darkness hid the people waiting on the Hoe. Those on the quay went slowly away, until only a watchman was left, marching up and down and swinging a horn lantern in his hand. Sailors came and drew up the landing stairs and secured them outside the railing. The door in the waist, through which so much cargo had been stowed, was closed with a squeaking of wooden pegs, and then there was a thud and a heavy bar dropped across it.

When all the colonists had been haled below into the common cabin for instructions and supper, Humphrey was still on deck, munching his meat and bread. He ate contentedly, with small bites and slow chewing. Now the ship was ready to sail and no one else could come or go. In a little while, only a few more hours, *The Lion* would up-anchor and be away.

After he had eaten, Humphrey lay down in his retreat, stretching his arms above his head as far as they would go. He rolled over and back again, like a cat, feeling ease spread through his whole body.

Tomorrow Eleanor would lay the cool tips of her fingers against his cheek in that pleasant way she had and she would probably say, "I knew you could do it." He himself had not been sure all the time, that he could.

The stars above the Devon coast were very bright tonight, he thought. Were they always like that in Maytime? Would they seem as close and as glittering in the sky above the New World? It would be a while before he found that out. The sailors were saying it would take two months and more to reach their chosen place. He would not mind.

The ship rocked a little with the motion of the water and the sails, already set to take the first blow of wind in the morning, blotted out the stars and Humphrey slept, with his hand clasping the pendant of a chain he wore round his neck, inside his jacket. It was his most precious link with home. It had been his mother's, the one thing he had allowed himself to bring beside his birthday gold pieces.

When he woke he found himself sitting up straight. His hand felt the rough surface of a blanket. Someone had covered him in the night. He listened. There was shouting on the quay.

"Ahoy there! Ahoy *The Lion!*"

Humphrey got up and walked softly across the deck to the railing. Two people stood on the quay beside the watchman, who held his lantern high. He cupped his other hand round his mouth, making ready to shout again.

The latecomers wore traveling cloaks and one had saddlebags across his arm. That one Humphrey knew well. It was his uncle, Jeremy Hall!

CHAPTER 3

Eight Bells

H UMPHREY'S heart raced. He had an impulse
to cross the deck behind him, leap the farther rail and swim quietly ashore, but his
mind said wait. So he watched the three on the
quay and even grinned a little at the way his
uncle threw the saddlebags on the stones and
stamped about.

Then, out of the shadows on deck, Humphrey
saw a light appear from an opened panel of a lantern like the watchman's. A quiet voice, clearly
heard in the still night, said, "Hist, yonder. I am
officer of the watch. 'Tis almost eight bells. D'ye
then want to wake up all that's aboard?"

"Yes," said Jeremy Hall, coolly, "if it takes that many to give me my rights."

"Rights! Who are you? What could you be wanting?"

"My nephew," Jeremy growled. "Hand him over. I know he is there."

"Who are you? What's your nephew's name?"

"I'm Jeremy Hall from York. The boy is called Humphrey Hall. I've a sheriff here with a warrant that proves my right to take him away. I am his guardian and I can't stand here all night talking. It has cost me a pretty tax in horseflesh to get here in time. Let down the stairs and help me aboard. I'll find him for you."

"You might and you mightn't. There is no Humphrey Hall on our lists."

Jeremy was almost dancing now. He shook his fist in the direction of the deck lantern. "Show me your face, you blackguard. I'll know if you are lying to me. I say, throw me a rope down. I'll not wait for stairs."

"Ye can see better by daylight. Wait until morning."

Humphrey let his breath go all the way out. *The Lion* would be gone by daylight.

"A candle will do me to scan your precious lists. Hand me aboard, I say!"

"I'll not, without the captain's order, and Master Stafford's asleep."

"Call Ananias Dare, then. I'll take his word."

The officer of the watch went away, and the low rumble of Jeremy Hall's complaint was the only sound, though Humphrey thought the beating of his own heart must be as loud.

When Ananias appeared on the deck, wrapped in his traveling coat, Uncle Jeremy had just shouted again, "Ahoy *The Lion!* What's the delay?"

Ananias answered in a friendly voice, "Ahoy yourself, Jeremy. Have you decided to go with us? Have you brought Humphrey too?"

"You know I haven't," said Jeremy, rudely. "I've come to take Humphrey home. I'll teach the young fool to run away and spoil my . . ."

"But Humphrey is not here. I swear to you I haven't seen him. I hope he is not in trouble somewhere."

"He's in trouble with me, and you are too, if you sneaked him off to London with you. I know he was making for this ship."

Ananias Dare's pleasant voice changed. It was crisp and his words were plain ones.

"No, I didn't, but you make me wish I had. Indeed you do. You don't own that boy, either as uncle or guardian. If he were here I wouldn't give him up now, nor let the captain. On my word, I wouldn't. But on that same word, I swear again that he is not here."

"Have you read the ship's list?"

"I have."

Jeremy stooped for his saddlebags. With never a thank-you nor good wish for Ananias' venture, nor a backward look at the ship, he said, "Come along, Sheriff. Though I hate his vitals, Ananias Dare is no liar. We're through here."

He strode off into the shadows of the quay with the sheriff at his heels.

Humphrey did not stir until the watch had escorted Ananias back to his cabin. Eight bells jangled from the forecastle. Four o'clock. The tide would soon be going out, possibly in an hour. He stumbled back to the blanket and was glad to wrap himself inside it, with its warmth between him and the deck. The dawn mists were chilly, and he wished Tobey were there to curl up against him. His heart still pounded like a drum beating inside him somewhere, and he drew long, shuddering breaths, trying to quiet it.

He was safe! Uncle Jeremy would be very angry when he got back to Gilling. If he should hurt old Tobey! "Oh, no, not that. I couldn't bear it." He had spoken aloud! Sobs shook him, then a long, shattering struggle without tears. Tobey! He beat the deck frantically with his fist, not minding now that he might be heard, and gasped, "Why did I do this? Tobey, I shouldn't have left you. I'll never have another dog like you, never! Oh, Tobey!"

Even grief was too much at last, and Humphrey slept with the fist relaxed into an open hand, palm down against the deck. When he woke again it was daylight, full, and the officer who had admitted him to the ship the previous afternoon stood looking down at him.

Humphrey sprang up, dizzily, out of the blanket and for a moment wondered where he was. He lurched and the man caught him and held him upright. His head ached and the bright sunlight hurt his eyes. There was something the matter with his feet, too. He couldn't get his balance. He blinked and squinted about. The ship was moving. There was water in every direction, no land in sight at all. *The Lion* had sailed while he slept. Then he remembered Tobey. He was sailing away from him. It was too late to go back. He would never know . . . He gulped and turned to the man.

"Did you . . .? Is there . . .? Have you any idea . . .?" he mumbled.

"One at a time, boy," said the seaman, grinning. "Yes, it was I who brought you the blanket. Yes, there is a place for you in the big cabin with the men. And I have an idea that Mistress Dare would be very happy to see you, but not looking as you do now. Come!"

Humphrey's head cleared a little, and he leaned over and picked up the blanket. It felt good to bend his stiff muscles. He stood upright and stretched mightily, then followed the officer down a steeper companionway into a large room on the deck below.

The place was dark with rich wood paneling, but the floor of wide boards was bare, as were the tables where a number of the colonists were eating. The sailor led straight through to a door in the farther wall, opening onto a small passageway. There were doors on either side of it, but the officer did not stop. He went ahead until he reached another opening at the end of the passage, and they stepped out into a large space which seemed to be at the stern of the ship. It was crowded with bunks in tiers. There were not enough portholes open and the odor of sleep and untidy human habits was heavy in the room.

The officer looked disgusted and opened a porthole and fresh, warm sea air rushed in. He turned to Humphrey.

"This is your berth, right here. And here's where you wash." He indicated a wooden bucket full of water standing on a rude bench. "You'll be the better for a bit of that. And you will keep your . . ." He looked blankly at Humphrey. "I remember now. You had no things with you yesterday. Had you no box? No other clothes?"

Humphrey looked down at himself, at the stains of rain and spilled food, the dusty boots. He was glad he had not demanded to be taken to Eleanor at once.

"My things are with the Mistress Dare," he said. "She was to bring them."

The officer said, "I see," as if he saw a great deal, and added, "Wait!" and disappeared through the passage door.

It was quiet in the room, with only the pleasant sounds of rushing wind and the sea outside. Humphrey stripped off his jacket and cambric shirt and turned to the bucket of water. He could clean himself while he waited. He had no doubt that the officer had gone to send someone with his clothes.

Then he heard a child's voice say, "Where did you come from?"

"York," said Humphrey, dully, without thinking about his answer, and then he straightened up, away from the bucket, and looked around to see where the child was. Two bright eyes were looking at him from a top bunk, near by.

"What's your name?"

"Must I have one?" Humphrey asked. He turned to the bucket again.

"Everybody has a name," said the child. "Mine is Georgie Howe, though you didn't ask me."

"Should I have asked you?" said Humphrey.

"Everybody does," said the little boy. "Because of my father."

"What's wrong with him? Is he in jail?"

"Oh, no, he didn't do anything bad. But his name is George, too."

"Oh, I see," said Humphrey. "Big George and Little George. Why don't you get up?"

"I'm up already but I can't get down."

Humphrey walked over and held up his arms. "You're a funny boy. If I hadn't come, you would have been up all morning and not down to breakfast. There!"

He swung the child to the floor, and they stood eying each other without another word until there was a sound of voices in the passage and Ananias came in, followed by two sailors carrying Humphrey's boxes.

Ananias said, "If your Uncle Jeremy could see you now!" And to the sailors, "There, set them down. Fine. Thank 'e, lads."

"How did you do it, boy? You and Eleanor together?" He was grinning approval. "Fool Old Jeremy?"

"You helped," said Humphrey, "last night."

'Nias looked pleased. "Story around already, is it?"

"I was there," said Humphrey, gravely, feeling his heart begin to thump again, remembering. "I was hid behind the skylight on the poop. I was sleeping there. The noise woke me and I listened."

"Poor Jeremy!" said Ananias, but he didn't sound sympathetic. "Now he will never be any greater, at Court or anywhere else."

Ananias changed his voice in a good imitation of Jeremy's best manner. "M'nephew, the Baronet Gilling," he mimicked. Then he laughed heartily, while Georgie stared at him.

Humphrey said quietly, "But I will have another manor to manage the way I like, one day, in the New World."

"If you don't get rich first with your share of the gold we shall find, and come sailing back to England to oust Old Jeremy from your lands."

"Gold? I?"

"That's the agreement. Sir Walter is keeping only one-fifth for himself, though he is financing the venture. Four-fifths is ours, the colonists'."

"If we find any . . ." said Humphrey slowly. "The land will be enough for me. Land that I have worked and seeded. Food that I have raised myself."

Ananias looked at him and shook his head. "You'd have had a sorry time at Court, with those ideas, fellow-me-lad. You will indeed be better off with us."

Georgie came a little closer. The child was fully dressed in plain clothes, which looked as if they had been slept in. He might be as much as five years old, not more, Humphrey decided. He looked a little like a girl, too, with those thin locks of yellow hair hanging limply way below his ears.

"Why do you wear a ring that way?"

Humphrey's hand flew to the chain around his neck. He had not meant his keepsake to be seen.

"It was my mother's, Georgie. It is as beautiful as she was, so I like to keep it near my . . . my heart. See!"

He held it closer for the little boy to look at.

It was a heavy silver ring, richly worked, holding an enormous square-cut amethyst, which winked in a dozen shades of violet and purple in the May sun.

"I'd be careful with that if I were you, Humphrey," said Ananias, "and please hurry now. Eleanor is impatient to see you."

He turned to Georgie. "Come along, young feller. Let's find your father. He should look after you better."

The cabin under the poop, the one with the skylight, had been given to the women, Humphrey found, and Eleanor was resting there when he made his manners later in the morning. It felt good to call on a lady again, dressed in his best doublet with puffed sleeves, carrying a hat and wearing proper shoes instead of riding boots. The Mistress Dare was pleased at Jeremy's outwitting. "I knew you could do it," she said.

When they reached the open sea nearly everyone was sick. Then the flyboat which had been sent along for protection in emergency was left behind in the Bay of Portugal. Now they would be an easier prey of any marauding Spaniard.

" 'Tis the navigator's doing. He give 'em the slip, I'll warrant."

"He wouldn't!"

"Oh, wouldn't he? He'd like a Spaniard to board us."

"But Simon Ferdinando is a Portygee."

"An' I'll wager he's in the pay o' Spain."

"When he's a Patentee of the new colony? Along of Governor White and 'Nias Dare and the rest?"

"A name to hide under. He was with Grenville two years back and made a good thing out o' that, too." The speaker winked. "Word gets around."

Humphrey heard and asked, "What if a roving Spanish man-o'-war should appear?"

The sailors laughed. One said, "Let it!" Another, "We'll board it, t'other way round. A right rich prize we'd get, gold and jewels, a share for every man, and a few dead Spaniards, too."

Gold! It was on every man's tongue and in every man's mind, the one thing on which all agreed, the last topic at night after day-long consideration, unless Tom the Lute was off duty.

He was a Welshman from the west country, and no one seemed to know him by any other name. It did not matter. He had a lute which he kept carefully in a case in his sea chest when he was at work. At night he played what the sailors asked for, chanteys, ballads, London street songs. He could lead them all.

There was one tune which became Humphrey's favorite of all the long list strummed out under the summer stars with the low, growling accompaniments of the sailors' voices beneath the plucking of the lute strings. Tom said it was new in London.

"Greensleeves was all my joy,
    Greensleeves was my delight,
    Greensleeves was my heart of gold,
        And who but Lady Greensleeves?"

There were eighteen verses and always at the
end the refrain, "And who but Lady Greensleeves?" The voyage could last a year and
Humphrey wouldn't mind if that music were
part of it.

"Greensleeves was all my joy." He went down
the companionway to bed one night, humming,
and did not notice the man standing in the
shadow at the foot. He jumped when a hand was
laid on his arm and a voice said softly, "You
wanted to be useful. There is something only
you can do. I will come for you when all is quiet.
Don't go to sleep."

It was the ship's officer who had befriended
him. But there was no friendliness in his voice
now.

CHAPTER 4

Gold

S OMETHING only you can do." There had
been warning in the officer's hard voice but
Humphrey was more curious than frightened, and it did not occur to him to disobey. He
lay down on his bunk, fully dressed, to wait.
What could it be? So far no duty had been as-
signed him. His presence on the ship had been
accepted, apparently without any argument. No
doubt 'Nias had seen to that. But the voyage had
been very dull, not at all exciting as he and
Eleanor had expected it to be.

Most of the colonists had settled into a daily routine. The women had numberless odd duties that housewives always seemed busy about, wherever they were. Governor White called frequent meetings with the Patentees. The spinster, Margaret Lawrence, had begun a school for the children, fat little Amby Viccars, Tommy Archard and Bobby Ellis, still babies really, with Georgie Howe alone of his age between them and Johnny Pratt, who was eleven.

Pastor Brooke held services, regularly, matins and evensong, which the women attended faithfully and more than a few of the men.

Lying rigid in the dark, Humphrey reviewed his own part. He had not even been considered worthy of scrubbing decks when a sickness broke out among the sailors and some of the colonists had been told off to help the seamen. Only he, neither child nor grownup, had had nothing to do, nothing except listen to the endless plans of boasting adventurers for making themselves wealthy in Virginia. Maybe this summons meant he could still prove himself on the ship. But why must it be done stealthily?

Midnight sounded from the forecastle and still Humphrey waited. He eased his stiff position and must have dozed a little, then, for he had no warning of the hissed whisper which told him the moment had come.

"Get up quickly and follow me."

The way led upward, going softly and scarcely breathing, to a small cabin aft, built cunningly into the curve beneath the bowsprit. It was a sumptuous place for one person. For the five already gathered and the two newcomers there was no comfort at all. The air was stifling as soon as the door was closed.

Against the longest wall of the three a bunk bed was draped in silk, hung from a ring in the ceiling, like a tester. The lions of England were embroidered in gold on the soft folds which were tied back with gilt cords.

There was only one chair, of heavy dark oak, with a high back. It was set behind a small table which held a pair of smoking candles. On a wall bracket above it stood a tall shining silver goblet, richly chased.

The man who sat in the chair was Simon Ferdinando, the Portuguese navigator. Humphrey had not yet seen him as close, but there was no mistaking the man's swarthy skin and rich dress. His face glistened with sweat, and there were little drops of it like tiny jewels caught in the hairs of the fashionable, sharply pointed beard.

The other men stood. Hunched miserably together, as far from Simon as the tiny space would allow, were two of the most uncouth of all the colonists. George Howe was there, too, an uncomfortable third. He flushed and started to speak and stopped when Simon glared.

Tom the Lute was the other man, lounging easily in a corner. He winked amiably when he met Humphrey's eye. What was the lute player doing here, in such company? Why was he himself here, Humphrey wondered. What did the whole thing mean? He began then to have his first doubts.

Simon spoke his name softly, and Humphrey turned back to look at the navigator, who had lifted a hand from which lace ruffles fell away, in a mock salute. White teeth and full red lips, veiled only a little by the candle smoke, showed against the blackness of the fine beard when he spoke.

"So, we are met, Master Thomas Humphrey Hall, Baronet of Gilling," he said. But there was no respect in his voice for an ancient title.

He looked then, contemptuously, at the officer. "You have brought me the boy. Why do you tarry?"

"For my promised reward, Simon, as well you know. I want it while we both have witnesses."

"You will get it, fellow. Have no fear. But later, later. I'm busy now."

The ship's officer took a step forward, until there was only the table between them, and he leaned above the lowering candles until he was in danger of a good scorching. He pounded the table with the flat of his hand.

"Now!" he said. "I want the gold now, Simon, the good, smooth feel of the pieces in my hand. I did not know the degree of the prize I had when I hid the lad aboard. Had it been my watch when his uncle arrived, searching, you'd

have seen neither of us on this voyage. Pay me
now, Simon, before I raise my price. Give it to
me in good English florins, none of the stuff you
get from your Spanish masters."

Simon shot to his feet and clutched the throat
of the officer, but Tom was there, and Humphrey, separating them and drawing the sailor
back to the door. Was he mad, to speak so to the
powerful navigator?

Another presence, fear, had crept into the
room to make an eighth. There was no longer
enough air, and the men held their aching lungs
suspended, waiting for what would come next.

Simon sat down, breathing heavily, and they
watched his hand inside his coat. But it was
neither dagger nor pistol which he drew out.
Gold pieces fell from a purse onto the table, and
the officer scooped them up avidly before he fled.
Humphrey had time to think, with the part of
his mind that was not bewildered, that they set
small worth on a fourteen-year-old boy. But if
he understood what he had just seen, he had
been sold, like any slave, because one man had
found out about the lands in Yorkshire.

"You will all forget what you have seen this
evening, except that we now have another we
can trust," Simon growled. He leaned from his

chair and blew out one of the candles. "If not, pfft, like that, he is gone. But I have made a good investment, I think." He grinned again. "As good a bargain as others I have made. Better, perhaps. Your debts were small."

The men looked at their feet again. Taken out of debtors' prison. Humphrey thought, to be haled off as colonists, but Simon's not Sir Walter's. In the pay of Spain? Certainly in Ferdinando's power. There was that gossip about his loyalties, which the sailor had dared mention.

"Now then, hark ye!" Simon's voice was smooth and silky again. The snuffed candle had not been replaced. Humphrey shivered. The unseen presence in the room had not left with the officer.

"I am changing some of the earlier plans and you, my trusted friends, should learn of it and be prepared." One could see the sneer in the flashing smile. "I intend to land this shipload of dolts on that island which Captain Barlow visited two years gone. It will change many things, I have no doubt," he even rubbed his hands together in prospect, "and I will not lose."

"But, Sir," said Humphrey, boldly, stepping forward, "Sir Walter has bonded you to land us up the Chesapeake and establish for him the

City of Raleigh in Virginia. That I know from the Dares."

Simon glared at the interruption. "Have I not heard it, too, from Raleigh himself, in unlimited detail? One may listen and not agree. I do not. It is too far from the coast. Why should I lose time navigating an unknown inland water with the season as far advanced as it shall be, when we arrive? Why should I, when I can be at more profitable business elsewhere?"

No one answered. From the table drawer Simon took out a map, and held it up for them to see. He pointed to a coastal spot with his long forefinger. "Here is that island I mentioned, Roanoke. We are to stop there first and see how fifteen men, left last year by Sir Richard Grenville, are faring. His earlier hundred sailed home. What is more simple than ending this voyage at Roanoke? Possibly you, too, will get sick of it and return to England also, but not before you have found gold for me. Because you will not be inland, it will then be the more easily collected by Spain. Altogether a vast saving for me in time and exertion. The Chesapeake indeed!"

Humphrey felt little fine prickles at the edge of his hair, above his jacket collar.

"I will instruct you what to do when a Spanish ship comes," said Simon, continuing his planning aloud.

Someone coughed and the quarter-hour sounded, muffled by the thick door.

"One will come," Simon added, confidently.

Sweat started in the palms of Humphrey's hands. What could he do to stop that firm, evil voice? Blow out the other candle? Push the table against the great chair and pinion Simon there? Would one of these cowards help him take a prisoner? The filthy, scheming traitor! Taking English money to keep *The Lion* on her course and meanwhile plotting for Spain. He took another half-step forward, felt eyes, and saw Tom's head, slowly motioning him to stay as he was.

"It is not meant for the English to have a successful colony on Roanoke or elsewhere in the New World," said Simon, as if he were a soothsayer, and oddly, at such a moment, Humphrey could remember a country fair at home, and a fortuneteller who had promised him adventure. How had that gypsy known?

"Not while Spain has power to prevent." Ferdinando gestured with a graceful hand to the shining silver goblet behind him. "That power has been used before. Sir Richard Grenville thought the Indians stole this cup from him. It was I. But his men punished a tribe and burned their village and cornfields, and they are now sworn enemies of England. It was Towaye's tribe, one of these two Indians aboard us, and he does not yet know. When he does find out!" Simon laughed, gloatingly. "It was made so easy for me, and you, too, are going to make other things easy."

He turned to Humphrey. "As for you, my fine young jackanapes, you are in favor with these stiff-necked Patentees. Though I also am one, they tell me nothing of any value. You, now, are to practice the art of spying on this ship. I want to know all the plans you hear, since you are so much in the confidence of the Dares." There was the sneer again. "Perhaps, in the course of your observations, you may note who are my other friends in the company. Not all were here to-night. And mark me, if you fail in anything, I can still get some slight return on my invest-ment. I can take you back to your uncle in York-shire."

Simon's slender, fine-fingered hand made a fist on the table. "As for that man John White, he's an irritating fellow, never in agreement with anything. But he would defend the colony if a

Spanish ship came, so it is best that he return to England, with me. It will come about. You will see."

He let them go, then. Nothing must spoil his plans, he insisted. Queen Elizabeth had refused to marry Philip of Spain. His people and their friends—Simon had given them his ugly grin again—meant it should cost her dear.

After that night Humphrey was sharply aware of things he had not noticed before. Who talked with whom. Where they sat to eat. Where they disposed themselves on deck during the long warm evenings. Who might those others be who were in the employ of Simon and through him, of Philip of Spain? He scarcely dared speak to any but the children.

Though Tom the Lute tried several times, Humphrey refused to talk to him. His own joy in Greensleeves was gone. It mentioned gold, which Tom was probably using as a signal of some sort to the other plotters. How could he, a traitor to England, hang about the children and play tunes for their games, as he did, whenever he was off duty in the daytime?

One night after the ship was quiet, Humphrey knew that someone was standing by his bunk. Now what? It was only George Howe.

"Please listen to me, Master Humphrey," he said in a low, strained voice. "I can't sleep. I got to talk. I just come from a buryin' . . . please God ye don't ever have to look on one, at sea. 'Twas one of the sick crew. Leastways, that's what Simon said, but I think, Master Humphrey, oh, watch yerself, lad . . . I think ye won't ever see that officer again, the one that . . ."

Humphrey said, "What? Simon wouldn't dare . . ."

"There's nothin' he'd stop at. Ye saw that silver cup. I could tell more, but I daren't. I'm no jailbird, Master Humphrey, but that man's got a hold on me and I can't break loose, not 'til we get to Virginia anyway. It looks like I'm not a good father, but I can't have Georgie round these chaps I have to stay with. Please keep'm in sight for me? Please, will ye do't?"

Humphrey promised and lay down again, but he could not sleep. The horror of George's story gripped him. So Simon would even kill if somebody got in his way! For a few frantic moments he wished he were back in York. He had left a comfortable home, and his dog and somewhat of peace. Perhaps he might have persuaded Uncle Jeremy, in time, to let him . . . His plain voyage was turning out differently, after all. It was not a pleasant difference. It would have been better not to be useful. But there was something else only he could do. That was to find a way to save himself and the rest from Simon's power.

He was called to the navigator's cabin only one time more before the voyage was done. He stood quietly while Simon looked him over and then answered his question.

"There is nothing to report, Sir," he said. "I have not heard anything about new plans. The Patentees do not speak of them openly."

"You happen to be right," said Simon, still staring at him. "I have had you watched. You people from Yorkshire have a way of telling the truth. It is a dull way to live. What a crowd this is! Matins and mating and music . . . Bah!"

CHAPTER 5

The Abandoned Fort

HUMPHREY leaned against the ship's rail one morning, in almost the same spot where he had stood the night before *The Lion* left Plymouth. He had thought then that he was in trouble. But at the same time he had hoped, if he sailed at all, to be a free man. Now he was only in Simon's power instead of Uncle Jeremy's. This present worry was far worse, though. It did not concern him alone. When the safety of others was threatened, he could not keep it to himself. There was no use denouncing Simon to the Patentees. He had no proof. There was only his

word against Ferdinando's. Who else was wise
enough to help him? Pastor Brooke?

Sir Walter trusted the pastor greatly, had
urged his coming so that the Church might be
established in Virginia. It had even been
planned, so Eleanor said, that Manteo, the elder
and more friendly of the two young red men
aboard, should be baptized by him as soon as
they reached the new land.

A shadow fell at Humphrey's feet and a voice
said, "Look at the water. From the back no man
can see the mouth." It was Manteo.

"You speak English well, Manteo," said Humphrey, "better than Towaye."

"Ah, the great Captain Barlow taught me,
and I had the desire. Towaye did not."

Manteo had been friendly from the first moment Eleanor had made them known to each
other, but Towaye had constantly remained
aloof. Humphrey spoke of that now.

"He is not of my tribe. We are Croatans of
the Algonquins. Towaye does not like the English. He did not want to sail to England. You
have a trouble, too, young chief, and not even
the charm you wear drives it away."

"My charm is only an old ring of my mother's
and I have said nothing about it nor of a trouble."

"Your hand goes to the charm, often. It is the red man's way to feel what is inside the mind. You understand that?"

"A little."

"Later, when you visit my country, I will show you how the red man knows."

"I will like that, Manteo. We will be stopping in your country, a long time, if the navigator does what he threatens . . ." Humphrey gasped and looked at the Indian. There was a gleam far back in Manteo's eyes, his way of smiling. "I am afraid of him, Manteo."

"Yes," said the deep voice. "The white boy has fear but is not a coward. Tell me your fear and it will be less because I will have part of it."

Except for a few guttural exclamations, Manteo said nothing until Humphrey had finished his story. "I will not spy on my own people, Manteo."

"He will not kill you," said the Indian. "You are worth more to him alive. There is your uncle who might pay him more gold."

The gleam which appeared in Manteo's eye then was not amusement. Humphrey was startled. Even his voice was different when he said, "I heard about the cup in England. That punishment was a wrong to all Indians. He must not glory in it long. Somehow the cup must be stolen again. That will not be a wrong, I think."

"No," Humphrey agreed, "but how can it be done?"

"The chance will come," said Manteo, sternly.

They both looked quietly at the sea. It was true, as Manteo said, Humphrey thought. A trouble shared was less heavy.

"How can I make a farm on an island, Manteo?" he asked, then. "There won't be room. We have over one hundred colonists, all these you see on the ship."

The amused look came back to the red man's dark eyes. "There is room," he said. "It is a large island. There is also the mainland. My country spreads many leagues to the west. We come to my island, Croatan, near Roanoke in summer only, for the fishing. That was how I first saw the great Captain Barlow."

In late July *The Lion* anchored at dawn one morning off that fair island, Roanoke, praised by Captain Barlow. It lay in a sound, reached after the ship passed beyond breakers through an inlet in the low coast.

The colonists sat to breakfast early, because the Patentees were anxious to go ashore and meet Grenville's men. Other than that, the day was begun in the same orderly fashion as when they were at sea.

Into this peaceful domestic routine Simon Ferdinando came striding, followed by Captain Stafford. He was scowling, and the captain looked worried. Everyone stopped eating. Simon had never honored them so, before. Was something wrong with the ship? People jumped up and food basins were overturned, which frightened the children. The soft voices of the mothers soothing them were interrupted by the announcement the navigator had come to make.

"I am not taking this ship farther. By night-fall every stick of your possessions must be set ashore. Englishmen have lived on this island before. What they could do, you can. Prepare to disembark immediately."

He turned to go, still followed by the distressed captain, but John White was blocking the door.

"What is the meaning of this, Sir?" he demanded. "You are a Patentee. Surely you could have discussed this with the rest of us. It is an outrage. You promised Sir Walter . . ."

Simon's roar of laughter drowned the rest of the Governor's words. "Raleigh is in England. We, you, are here. The ship will not sail without me, you agree. And I do not propose to sail it to the Chesapeake, an inland water I do not know, when this island is good enough for you."

"But, man, we have our orders," John White protested.

"And I am giving you others," said Simon. "It is too late in the season for me to go farther. Get these people ashore."

The navigator thrust the Governor aside as if he had been a chair in his way, went out and closed the door. It sounded familiar to Humphrey, but Simon had omitted the part about Spanish ships.

Nothing more was eaten of that meal. The women were frantic, partly at the thought of living on an island, and partly at the need for speed in packing up. The men were angry and held a meeting, but there was nothing anyone could do. Simon had retired to his cabin and remained there, shut away from all arguments and pleadings.

The sailors had had their orders, too, for by the time the colonists had climbed to the deck, the men were preparing the ship's small boats for transferring the goods to shore. They looked even smaller than they really were, from the height of the ship's deck down to water level, and the women stormed Simon's cabin then, but even that did no good.

In the midst of the confusion, the hurried packing, the pleading, the children's wails, Manteo stood quietly at the ship's rail. There was no sign of Towaye. "Gone," said Manteo, when Humphrey asked. "He climbed down by a rope and swam ashore as soon as the sails were folded. He is with his people now."

"And they are not with yours?"

Manteo shook his head. "They live at the other side of Roanoke."

Humphrey followed the White party when it

came their turn and sailors rowed them ashore, with the cradle riding on the boy's knees. The confusion on the beach was as bad as that on the ship. People and goods and animals in a strange mixture and the hot July sun beat down on all.

John White did not see any of it. With one foot still in the small boat, he was calling to Dion Harvie, already landed.

"I say, where are Grenville's men? Haven't you seen anything of them? Why aren't they here to greet us? Surely they will have seen the ship by this time. It is almost noon and we have been here since early morning!"

Dion shook his head. "I'm afraid, Sir, I had more thought for helping my wife. She is worried about her geese. This is a hopeless thing at the moment. But it does seem strange that someone hasn't appeared. What do you suggest?"

"A search, at once," said John White, shortly. He waved his hand at the scene. "This will straighten out. It's only another Plymouth Hoe. Come along. Let the women tend the goods. 'Nias!"

Humphrey stood by, to see what the Governor would do. He could see log houses among the trees higher up on the slope of the island. But there was no smoke coming from their chimneys.

Roger Pratt, another Patentee, arrived then from the ship and he was hailed to join the discussion. 'Nias turned to Humphrey.

"Come along, boy!" he said. "We are going with the Governor to look up Grenville's men, and you may be useful."

Humphrey was beginning to dislike that word, but he'd be one of the first to see the older colonists, he realized, and he followed the four men up the beach path toward the houses. There was a wonderful smell in the warm air and as they went he saw what it was.

"Look, 'Nias! Grapes!"

He stopped to pick a handful of the heavy fruit, yellow and dripping with juice, which grew on low vines everywhere, in places almost at the water's edge.

But the men were not interested, and Humphrey had to hurry to join 'Nias again. Something must be wrong if they didn't care about fresh fruit after the long voyage. It did seem queer those fifteen men hadn't yet showed themselves.

They discovered why, at the first house. It had not been lived in for a long time. The chinking had begun to fall out of the log walls. The wilderness was pushing inside. Vines and creeping plants draped the doorways and empty windows. Melons were ripening in the heavy vegetation.

A little farther on, a deer bounded out of the open doorway of another house and disappeared in the forest. After the sounds of its crashing through the undergrowth had died away, the silence of the place was ghostly.

They looked at each other, the four men and the boy, and John White said, in a low voice as if he were in church, "Grenville's men are not here. They haven't been for months. It is plain from the condition of these buildings."

"Indians, Sir?" 'Nias' lips barely formed the words.

"Who can tell?"

"Look!" said Humphrey, gesturing. "They tried to build a fort."

He walked ahead now, toward the ruined fortification beyond the last house. It seemed to have been mainly a low earthwork, higher on the east side, toward the sea. The entrance was near the houses. Small rounded embrasures could be traced at the corners, as if a greater protection had been arranged for a guard, standing regular duty.

"It was well planned," said John White. "A pity it did not help them."

"They may have gone away in search of food," said Dion Harvie. "We may find them yet."

"But Grenville said he left supplies sufficient for two years. That was only a year ago," Governor White objected. He shook his head. "I cannot understand it."

Humphrey thought, Now they will beg Simon to take us all back, and we will have to get all that stuff loaded on the ship again. If fifteen men couldn't last a year, how could a whole colony exist?

He was surprised when 'Nias said, squinting up at the sun, "I think we had better be getting back to the others. We must plan how we are going to sleep tonight. I don't suppose Ferdinando would consent to hanging about a bit and let the women go back aboard to sleep?"

"The blackguard!" said John White. "How he has tricked us, and Raleigh! I do not understand that, either."

"We may never find out any of these answers," said Dion, "and I hope the absence of these men isn't going to upset people so we can't organize properly. After all, we came here to make a home."

"We will make it," said 'Nias, striding out ahead on the path.

Humphrey longed to speak, but couldn't decide that it was the right time, particularly if Ferdinando might delay, and so endanger his own chance of remaining. Now that he was here he meant to stay, if the others did.

The women were so intent on setting up their housekeeping that they didn't seem as frightened by the absence of the Grenville party as Dion had feared. They began on the houses, after looking skeptically at the vines and fearsomely at the dirt floors. It was warm work, Humphrey found, making himself useful at pulling away the heavy growth. The roots were deep.

Some old sails were commandeered from the ship to make a few tents until quarters for the single men could be built. The families were to have the houses and each would take in a few others. Axes rang in the woods that very afternoon where the Berry brothers had organized a working party. Henry's small anvil and bellows were carried up to the fort enclosure and left there, while he helped the carpenters.

Humphrey took a blanket to the warm sand to sleep that night, a short way from the rest. He hoped that the promise given George Howe on shipboard would not extend to the land. Surely he couldn't be expected to look after the child all the time. He had too much else to do. But he had scarcely spread the blanket in a good spot when Georgie appeared, looking a little like a puppy, ready to wag his tail if he got a kind word.

"My father said I was to sleep where you do, Humphrey."

Humphrey groaned, and rolled over. "Come onto my blanket, then, but promise me not to talk. I want to think."

Georgie curled down as close to Humphrey as

he could get. "What have you got to think about, Humphrey? England? I don't like this place. Something big, with shiny eyes, jumped out of the bushes. It ran away, but I'm scared, Humphrey."

"Did the big thing's eyes shine up high or down low?"

"Up high, Humphrey. Higher than me."

"Probably it was one of the deer we saw this afternoon. It was afraid of you."

"That big thing?"

"That big thing. What a silly you are!"

Humphrey reached for the grapes hanging just above their heads and popped one in Georgie's mouth. "There, eat that! You never had grapes growing above your bed in England, I'll wager. This is a wonderful place. You will like it better tomorrow. Go to sleep now. I want to think about the farm I shall have."

He turned young Georgie over on his stomach, making him lie perfectly flat, and rubbed his back, up and down, in an even motion until the frightened child slept. Humphrey smiled, remembering back rubs by his mother in Gilling.

The stars were close and the beach was still, except for the little lap, lap, lap of the water along the sand. Sir Walter might be disappointed in this site, Humphrey thought, but they could still establish the City of Raleigh, even if it had to be on an island. They were nearer to England here, and to help from passing ships. If any ships passed! English ones, certainly, not Spanish.

As for the gold! He hadn't thought to ask anyone what it looked like in its rough state, and he had been too busy all day to search for any, if he had. There would be plenty of time to find out later. He drew a deep, almost contented breath. In spite of Uncle Jeremy he had come to the New World, and this was his first night in it.

Out in the Sound the riding lights of *The Lion* repeated themselves in the tossing water. Why had the navigator delayed after he had been in such a hurry to get rid of the colonists? Had he put them off quickly so they could find him some gold to take back?

Faintly from the ship came a fine sweet thread of sound. Tom the Lute was singing "Greensleeves is all my joy."

A step sounded on the sand and Humphrey could make out, through the bushes, a lone woman walking slowly along the shore, looking steadily toward the ship. Someone was homesick, perhaps. She turned and in the starlight he saw the face of the spinster, Margaret Lawrence.

CHAPTER 6

The Cove

IN the morning Humphrey sent Georgie to play with the other children while he helped Eleanor, who was settling her family in the largest of the log houses, as befitted the Governor's position. The Widow Pierce was enjoying it, he could see, under her expressed disgust for the way the previous occupants of the place had treated it.

She was vigorously brushing the floor of the large main room with a broom made of fine twigs bundled together. She said, "Even a dirt floor can be made do, if it's taken care of."

Humphrey offered to finish the job. "No," she said, "you go and find me some of those grapes for our meal. The sun gives me a headache."

It was a pleasant errand, and while Humphrey hunted the biggest and ripest bunches, he kept an eye out for a small pool to use for his own washing place. Though he had never lived near the coast in England, he had noted such indentations in the shore line on his walk to Plymouth and hoped to find this one similar. The search led him farther than he meant to go and presently the ground sloped away to a narrow marsh which seemed to divide the island almost in two at that point.

He was turning back when there was a slight movement in the reeds and he heard a low groan. He laid his grapes on a clean stone and went cautiously forward in the direction of the sound. At the edge of the marsh, lying half out of the water, was George Howe, with a long arrow in his neck. His eyes were closed, but he was still breathing.

Humphrey knelt and touched his shoulder gently. "George, what has happened to you? What are you doing here?" Then he saw the rusty platter, with a single crab in it.

George opened his eyes. They were dull, but he was conscious. He said, painfully, "Take care . . . my Georgie. I tried. . . . Beware the Spanish, Mas . . . ter . . ." he gasped for breath, and then he raised his head and the last words whistled out, "They'll send a ship." Blood gushed from his mouth, and his head fell back on the crushed reeds. Humphrey straightened the body after pulling the feet out of the water.

It was only then that he thought to look about, but there was no sign except the trampled plants that another human being had been within miles of the marsh. Humphrey did not touch the arrow. He picked up the grapes and put them in his hat and plodded soberly back along the beach and up the slope to the houses. He must find Ananias and send the men to . . . What would happen to young Georgie now?

The colonists chose a high spot beyond the fort site near a clump of cedars for a burying ground, and that afternoon Pastor Brooke conducted a short service in the open.

When it was over, the Widow Pierce beckoned Humphrey to follow her. He was glad to go with her. All day Georgie, white-faced and silent, had clung to him, and no one had offered to help. Perhaps Eleanor had thought of something.

She had, indeed. Both boys were to live with the Dares. Eleanor sat in the large, swept room in one of her high-backed chairs and reasoned it out for them.

"The men's quarters will be no place for Georgie, and you, Humphrey, can be useful here. The Widow Pierce needs a man's help when 'Nias is so busy all the time."

Humphrey frowned at the word "useful," but Eleanor had as good as called him a man. She did not see the frown. She was holding out her hand to Georgie, who wore his tail-wagging look.

On the second morning following their first funeral Henry Berry stood awkwardly before Governor White in the main room of the Dare house where the family were still at breakfast.

He said, "Some of us think that what happened to Howe changes things some and we better start work on the fort, maybe?"

"Well, Berry, having a fort didn't seem to help Grenville's men. *The Lion* is still in the Sound. We can return to England."

"Begging your pardon, Sir, we can't back out now. This is a likely place. We've been here only two days, but already it looks different. Some of us want to be a mite forehanded and get at the

fort right away. That's all. Indians might think twice, had we proper defenses, before trying any tricks with us."

"You think they might? What do Manteo and Towaye say?"

Humphrey broke in, without asking permission. "Towaye went off to his people the first morning early, and he hasn't come near since."

"Why hasn't somebody told me of this? If it means he is not friendly, it could be highly significant." The Governor's voice was sharp. "Do you suppose it was he who . . . I mean could he have had a personal grudge against Howe?"

"Oh, no," said Henry, "and nobody meant

any harm, Sir, not telling you about Towaye. We had a lot to do."

"That's no excuse. It is disturbing news. I must speak to the Patentees." He drummed on the table with his fingers, as he always did when annoyed. "Do you think you and Mark Bennett could go ahead with the fort and the other buildings at the same time?"

"Give me some good men. Most of them don't rightly know just what they came for, out here to this colony. They talk gold so hard they can't see anything else needs to be done. Fall over them, they don't notice."

Governor White went with Henry to the door. When he came back he said, testily, "Why didn't the fellow come right out and say he couldn't stir some of these idlers to work until I ordered them to? They will get their orders. Gold! H'm! We might have found some up the Chesapeake."

The women cleared the table and disappeared with Georgie between them. They meant to cut his hair. Humphrey was making for the door to follow Henry Berry, when Governor White called him back.

"Sit down, Humphrey. I want to talk to you."

Humphrey sat again, wonderingly, on the edge of his chair. He hoped this wouldn't take

long. There was always fun around where Henry
Berry was, he decided. The Governor couldn't
have anything very important to say.

John White made a tent of his fingers and
tucked them under his chin. "Humphrey, I have
decided to send you back to England when *The
Lion* sails."

The room spun around and Humphrey
blinked and said, "But, Sir . . ."

"Now, now, I have thought it all through carefully. Your uncle is our neighbor in Gilling.
He is your legal guardian and I will not be a
party to hoodwinking him the way you have
done. Besides, you will be a good companion for
the little boy. I am sending Georgie Howe back
to his father's people."

Humphrey's heart was pumping blood so fast
he could scarcely breathe. He had never thought
of this possibility. Why had he himself been such
a child to think he could manage his own affairs,
that there would not always be a grownup
around with different ideas? He might be able
to thwart Simon's, but not this!

Pastor Brooke interrupted the silence that
fell at the end of the Governor's harangue, with
his "Good day to this house!" He almost filled
the doorway with his big body and hearty voice.

He was invited in and given a seat. He inquired after Eleanor's health and commended them for looking after young Georgie.

"It was the only decent thing to do at the moment," said the Governor.

He hadn't had a thing to do with it, Humphrey knew.

"It's a fine morning," ventured the pastor, looking from the Governor to Humphrey's glum face.

"Yes," said John White, vaguely, then he roused and seemed to have come to a decision.

What now, Humphrey wondered.

"Pastor, you are twice welcome this morning," said the Governor. "I have had to deal with a matter according to my best judgment and I need your help to convince this young man I am right."

"So?" said Pastor Brooke. "Is it then so serious?"

"You knew, of course," Governor White explained, "that Humphrey ran away from his home to join the ship. It was with my daughter's connivance, it is true. I understand that the only thing they didn't bring off was to smuggle Humphrey's dog along."

Humphrey's hands made fists, hid by the table.

The Governor could have left out that part, certainly.

"I have decided to send Humphrey back to his uncle. He can look after young Georgie Howe on the way. There are relatives in England who will welcome the child. I have made some inquiry."

Pastor Brooke looked from man to boy again. He asked, "What does Humphrey say? He is strong and will be a useful member of this colony. You can't . . . He will be a man and can bear a man's part in no time."

"Both boys have families, and children should be with their own people," said Governor White smoothly.

"True, true," the pastor murmured, "but not in all cases. Not, certainly, in Georgie's. Aged maiden great-aunts are not . . ."

The tone was mild but Humphrey looked up, hopefully. The Governor stirred in his chair.

"You must have some better reason for sending Humphrey home?" the pastor asked. "He had a good one for running away, I doubt not. He took some risks. He left his dog behind. Why did he do it? Merely for the adventure?"

Humphrey sprang up. "Nay, I will tell you, Pastor Brooke," he said. He jerked his jacket straight and smoothed his hair, and stood well away from the table.

"It was my uncle. He wanted me to go to Court, to be educated there and attend upon the Queen. He is powerful in York and he wanted . . . they called him ambitious. My people are of the land. We have much of it. I wanted to stay at home and learn to manage my own farms. But my uncle refused, so I ran away, hoping to have another manor here, one day."

Pastor Brooke looked at the Governor. "You would send him back, knowing that? I do not understand you, Sir."

Governor White flung a hand out, palm up, toward the pastor. "There is power in wealth. This uncle can make great trouble for . . . well, for all of us if we . . . when we return to England."

The silence descended again. The pastor rose to go. "I'm afraid I cannot advise you," he said stiffly.

"Wait!" John White rose, too. "There is another way. It means keeping Georgie, but that will please my daughter. If you would consent to teach Humphrey, teach him Latin and what you may know of court ways, there will be less trouble with the uncle when we do return."

Pastor Brooke said, "Latin is not easy, Humphrey."

"That does not matter, Sir," said Humphrey, stoutly, "if learning it lets me stay here."

"Come along, then. We will have your first lesson, forthwith, on the way to my room."

It was not until an hour later, when he had let Humphrey go, whooping up the hill to the fort, that the good pastor remembered his own errand of the morning. He had meant to ask the Governor where and when they proposed building a chapel for the colony. They should not wait too long before carrying out Sir Walter's wish for Manteo's baptism. The Indian was willing. It would be wise to hasten it in view of the fact that George Howe had been killed by an Indian arrow. Pastor Brooke did not believe it had been an accident nor yet a personal grudge.

Governor White had another caller that morning. He was conscious of a shadow in his doorway, darkening the room a little, and looked up to see Manteo standing there. He bade the young Indian come in.

"I have brought you my mother's invitation to visit my people," said Manteo. "It would be wise if the Governor and the Patentees made friends with the tribes, because visiting is better than killing. Croatan Island is not far. We will bring a boat. You will come?"

Governor White said, "I should like to be wise, Manteo. Thank your mother for me and say we will come. Only let us start our building first."

Manteo nodded. "That, too, is wise," he said and was gone and there was light in the doorway again.

At the time of the evening meal Humphrey turned up, completely disheveled, with the shorn Georgie at his heels.

"Where have you been?" Eleanor demanded crossly, as if Humphrey were only Georgie's age. She stood with her arms akimbo on her wide hips and looked them over.

"You'll not sit at my table like that, either of you. Ugh!" She put a hand to her nose and pinched the nostrils shut. "Where *have* you been? You . . . you . . . you reek."

Humphrey laughed. It felt good to be scolded in that fashion by a woman again. He had not had it for so long. Such a home feeling was worth the scolding.

He said, "It's only clean dirt, Eleanor. We've been up at the fort. It's the most exciting place. They dug up some things this afternoon that belonged to the first Grenville colony. 'Tis only sweat you smell." He took Georgie's hand. "Come on; we must go and wash."

He led the little boy down to the beach and headed for the rocky point beyond which lay the small sheltered cove that he had finally found the day after the funeral. It was at the opposite end of Roanoke from the marsh, near the inlet where *The Lion* had come in. He could feel already the refreshing water on his hot, dirty body and urged Georgie to hurry.

There was no need of haste. Standing on the sand beside the muddy, churned pool were two young Indians holding between them an enormous stone, poised ready to heave it, too, into the roiled water. One of them was Towaye.

The other, with even more princely bearing, in spite of his occupation, seemed Towaye's age. He saw Humphrey first and spoke to Towaye, and the rock slipped so that both leaped to escape its falling on their feet.

There was a bow slung on Towaye's back and he reached for it, but Humphrey said, "No, Towaye. You have done enough harm without killing. Why do you hate me so? The tide will come in and clean my pool, you must know. So why did you do this?"

Towaye said, "Towaye like to hate. Not just you. All white people. Not your pool. Mine, my island."

"But Manteo's people belong on the Sound, too."

Towaye spat. "Manteo! He white, too, inside. Towaye is red man, inside, outside."

Georgie had been clutching Humphrey's leg tightly, and the child was shaking all over. Humphrey pulled away the clinging hands and said, "Sit down. We will wait for the tide to clean the pool."

He leaned and began to undress Georgie. The strange Indian boy stared a moment and then leaped in the air as the first fingers of the racing water tickled his ankles. He landed running and Towaye was obliged to follow his friend, with a final black look at the two so calmly engaged with buttons and shirts on the beach.

Humphrey said, "Don't shake so, Georgie. Towaye just likes doing mean things. He was only showing off before his friend with that bow business. But we won't say anything to Eleanor about it, will we? Promise? Not until after the little baby comes, anyway, huh? We'll have a secret."

Georgie laughed shakily. "Just like the one with my father about the Spanish ship. He told me that it would come, and I must run and hide if it did." It was the first time he had spoken of his father.

Humphrey said, "Yes, now you have two secrets. That is enough for one little boy. There, the water is clean now. In you go. I'll hold you up."

So, had George Howe known something the rest of Simon's plotters did not? Why had he been killed? Should he, Humphrey, tell what George had said, when he died? That would not be betraying his own relation to Simon. Perhaps he should tell Manteo, first.

CHAPTER 7

The First Warning

THE colony was a week old when Manteo brought an enormous boat, a hollowed-out log, which would seat twenty men, to take Governor White and his party to the Indian camp on Croatan Island. They had gone perhaps two miles north when Manteo pointed out a thin drift of smoke on the other side of Roanoke. "It blows from Towaye's village," he said. There was little to mark the shore they were passing, but Humphrey saw one enormous rock to fix the spot in his mind, as Manteo had been teaching him to do. "The Indian way is to be on

watch, without seeming to be," the young chief
had said. "That is your safety."

Manteo's people were assembled in full welcome when the boat grounded on Croatan's
white beach. The women wore dresses made of
soft deerskin, loose-hanging and heavily fringed.
Their hair was worn in thick plaits down their
backs. Dogs barked. Children got in the way.

Humphrey knew almost at once which of the
women was Manteo's mother. Their faces were
very like. She motioned the whole party to follow her up to an open space in front of their

bark huts where an enormous feast was laid, meats, the fruits of sea and garden, cold and hot, dried and fresh.

When no one could eat any more, there were speeches made by the Governor and by Manteo's brethren, which he interpreted for each group. Then Governor White invited the chiefs to come to Roanoke the following week.

When it was time for the return journey all the Indians went again with them to the beach. Governor White was already seated in the boat and Humphrey was stepping in when Manteo said, "Wait. They have a gift for you."

He turned and there was a young girl tearing along from the bark huts with something which moved when she laid it carefully in her mother's outstretched palms. Humphrey's eyes widened and his own hands went out with no urging from Manteo, when the Indian woman offered him what she held.

Manteo said, "My mother thinks you very brave to leave your good dog in England and come to our country alone. So this little one is for you. I told her about your mother's ring and she says that He-Who-Wears-a-Charm shall always be welcome in the bark houses of the Croatans."

There was a lump in Humphrey's throat. He bowed gravely to Manteo's mother and held the puppy against his cheek for a moment to hide his joy. Then he moved the soft brown and white bundle to the crook of his left arm, where it settled confidently against him, trying to lick his fingers.

When they came into Roanoke water at early twilight, one of *The Lion's* small boats was seen pulling back to the ship. It was too far away to hail.

"Look!"

"Why is he alone? Hot work for one."

"Must have brought a message. Can *The Lion* be sailing at last?"

Without being asked, Manteo signaled his men to paddle a little faster.

"I say!"

There was a splash in the water near the lone rower. And another. Then Humphrey heard a buzzing sound, as if an angry bee were zooming by and somebody else said, "D'you see that?"

The men began twisting in their places and the canoe tilted and Manteo called out, a little sharply, "Sit!" But by that time everyone had seen the strong black arrow sticking in the wood at the prow of the log boat and still quivering.

"Not meant for us, surely," said the Governor. "But why does he want to pot the fellow in *The Lion's* boat?"

"Scare," said Manteo, briefly. "You, too."

"But we don't, not that easy," said Henry Berry. "Be glad to get ashore, though. Might find who shot."

"There is only one, or perhaps two," said Manteo, "and they can be far by the time we beach."

"Perhaps two." Towaye and his friend? Humphrey wondered and remembered at the same time that there had been no opportunity to tell Manteo about the threatened visit of a Spanish ship. There was plenty of time, though, with Simon still hanging about. Ah, what if he were leaving soon? What about the cup?

When they landed, Manteo said, "See to your women!"

"But what does it mean, Manteo?" Governor White asked.

"Scare," said Manteo again. "Towaye's tribe do not want white people on this island."

Humphrey waited until the men were out of hearing, and Manteo held his paddlers while they talked. "How will we get the great cup, if *The Lion* is preparing to sail?"

It was now almost dark, and Humphrey could not see Manteo's eyes, but there was guttural assurance in his answer. "If the Great Spirit wills, it will happen."

In the Dares's house the Widow Pierce was pouring doses into the children's open mouths while the mothers stood by to use force if they had to. Some was needed. Margaret Lawrence was there, too, but she was only wringing her hands and crying.

Above the din of the children's howls and gagging, Elizabeth Viccars was shouting, "Pox or flux, we'll all be down. Both are catching. There, swallow it, Amby, that's my little man."

Georgie moved out of line like a shot when he saw Humphrey.

"Humphrey's brought a dog!" he yelled. "Let me hold it!"

Eleanor tried to pull him back in line. "I don't want that old medicine," he screamed. "I want to hold the puppy."

Margery Harvie said, "Take the dose like a good boy, Georgie, and I'll give you a little goose for a pet."

Governor White thundered, "What *is* the meaning of this?"

Only Jane Pierce had courage to break the
awed silence. "It's the sailors, Sir," she said.
"All of them are down sick now, with the fever
that began on the voyage. That's why they have
not sailed. They sent and wanted I should come
out and dose the lot."

"You are not going," said Henry Berry.

The Widow gave him a look that sent him
back to the fireplace where Humphrey and the
other men stood watching. The odor of the nox-
ious medicine and the peculiar, strong sweat
of anxious people was heavy in the room.

"I sent a mixture," said Mistress Pierce,
shortly. "Pox or flux, 'twill do them good. You'd
all be better for a dose. I've plenty, full of the
good English herbs I brought with me."

"Not now, thank you," said Governor White.
"This is most unfortunate. I've invited all the
chiefs from the islands hereabouts to a meeting
next week. 'Nias! Harvie! Think this will make
any difference?"

There was no answer. Only the women and
children were still with him. The men, even
'Nias, were gone.

Eleanor hoped that Georgie would forget Mistress Harvie's promise, but the next morning he
insisted upon going to choose his pet. It was a

half-grown bird with a cross look, and a heavy
armful for the little boy. He promptly named it
Sir Walter and wouldn't change, even when they
assured him it was not a gander.

At home, he burst into the main room, set
his burden down and called the family to see.

"Now I've got a pet, too," he shrilled. "Where
shall I keep him?"

'Nias looked at Eleanor, stroked his chin
thoughtfully, and said, "The hearthstone is as
good a place as any, Georgie."

The Patentees decided not to tell their wives
anything about the warning arrows, not until
they had to. But the other men who had gone
to Croatan were able to put enough fear into
all the rest to speed work on the fortifications so
that Henry Berry had all the help he needed
there, at last.

He had planned a much better fort, one with
a high stockade and outside that a deep, wide
ditch, bridged only at the entrance.

"Indians can't climb up outside so easy,
mebby, did we have a valley all round," he explained, "and strength talks."

So did the skeleton, though silently. They
found it in the long grass when they began the
ditch. The news flew and everybody came run-

ning to the fort. No one in the colony worked that morning.

The bones had been found on the side toward the sea, where a man had fallen face down with arms outflung. The arrow which had killed him was still sticking in his frame.

They searched the spot all round, parting the spears of coarse grass with their hands, looking for any small thing which had belonged to him, a ring, or a shoe buckle, a coat button or some pocket trinket, that might tell whence he came. But there was nothing to identify him, nothing to show whether or not he had been one of Grenville's lost fifteen.

Later they held another service and gave George Howe a companion on the cedar knoll.

It was a relief to the women that they must plan for the living. "What shall we feed the Indians?" Eleanor demanded of her father at breakfast the next day. "After that feast they gave you, anything we do will look poor."

John White was embarrassed. "I didn't think about food. It's their friendship I'm after."

"Never knew a man yet wasn't friendlier if you fed him," said the Widow Pierce.

"Main thing is to get them here," said Henry Berry. He had stopped by with a question about

the new chapel and had been invited to eat. "A good look at that fort will be real quietin'."

"But we've got to plan a feast," said Ananias, firmly. "They will expect it. In England we wouldn't ask people to come for an all-day meeting and not give them something to eat."

"All day!" Eleanor exclaimed.

"Why not? What with speeches and bowing and scraping and pipe-smoking and eating and swearing eternal friendship? A whole day, easily. And what a day!"

The women looked at each other with raised eyebrows. Humphrey looked at the hourglass.

It was time for his Latin. He scooped up the puppy from the hearth and Georgie's goose hissed loudly.

"Ask Mistress Harvie to come and talk about the victualing," Eleanor bade him.

Humphrey grinned. "Maybe she will let you have her geese to roast."

John Brooke was smoking a long-stemmed clay pipe, packed with the newly discovered tobacco leaf. It had a pleasant fragrance. Humphrey wondered if he could grow it on his farm.

"Good day to you, Humphrey."

"Good day, Sir. I am sorry to be late. I had to do an errand for Eleanor about the feast."

Pastor Brooke eyed the puppy. "Do you think to mix dogs and Latin? Have you chosen a name for him yet?"

"I thought to call him Lion, Sir. After the ship. Do you mind if he stays? He's so little I hate to leave him. He knows me already. Do you think he looks like a hunting dog? I never saw this breed before."

"Nor I," said John Brooke. "But all dogs are hunters, in a way." He puffed thoughtfully. "What about this feast?" he asked.

"The Governor didn't think we needed to

have one and 'Nias said we did, so I thought maybe Mistress Harvie would give them her geese to roast and . . ."

"Oh, Humphrey, we couldn't allow that. Mistress Harvie wants to raise a big flock."

In a moment he reached for his hat. "Latin class is dismissed. Let's go see Henry."

They found him at his anvil inside the fort enclosure, making iron strap hinges for the heavy shutters in the chapel windows.

"Can you spare any men, Henry?" said the pastor, stepping inside. "The women need some fresh meat for this feast thing with the Indians. How about a hunt? Have you seen anything we might bag?"

Henry grinned. "They will all want to be spared for such, me included. I saw ducks flying over, this morning. Probably there's a feeding place down in George's marsh. Hear tell there's pig around, too, running wild from Grenville's time. For myself, some deer meat cooked our style would be real tasty."

Humphrey wondered if he could trust Georgie to look after Lion. He himself couldn't stay at home, not from this first hunt. The next moment he was flying along the path home, without a word to the puzzled pastor. He burst into the log house and found it full of women, the whole seventeen, met to talk about food. Margery Harvie was sobbing, wildly.

"Will somebody please look after my dog for me? I promised Eleanor he wouldn't be any trouble, but we're going hunting . . ."

"Hunting!" It was a sixteen-voice chorus.

"Yes, to get you something for your feast. Henry has seen ducks and there's deer and he thinks maybe we can get a wild pig. You'll have something to cook."

Somebody took Lion and somebody else said, "There, now, Margery, stop crying! You can keep your geese."

Manteo was coming up the beach path, carrying a large fish for his friend, the White Doe.

Humphrey said, "Oh, Manteo, must you go home at once? Do come with us." He explained their necessity.

Manteo's eyes gleamed. "I will come."

The hunting party was small. Henry Berry and his brother, Mark Bennett and two of his carpenters, 'Nias and Dion Harvie, Manteo and Humphrey. Henry took charge when they entered a faint trail which led into the woods beyond the cemetery knoll.

"Now I don't look for any trouble with a deer," said Henry. "They're so plentiful it should be like cutting the best one out of a herd of cows and helping ourselves. But pig is different, mind! You got to look out. Wild ones can be mean. Don't want anybody hurt."

Humphrey, following Manteo in the rear, thought the hurts might more likely come from Towaye, who seemed to know every thought in the colonists' minds. How had Towaye known so quickly that he had chosen the cove for his own? Didn't he do anything else but spy?

It was cool in the forest shade, and their eyes adjusted after a while to the different light. They came to a spring where deer were accustomed to drink, evidenced by the marks of their hoofs in the damp earth. Henry arranged hiding places, downwind, and they waited. It was his gun which brought down a fine young buck, and the carpenters who dressed the carcass at once and slung it on a sapling pole for easier carrying.

"Ducks can wait until tomorrow morning," Mark said. "That's the best time, sneak up on their feeding place. If we can get a good porker, those Indians will be our friends for life."

He had scarcely spoken when there was a crashing sound in the bushes ahead and a pig broke cover and ran across an open, grassy slope directly in front of them.

Manteo said "Faugh!" and lifted his bow. 'Nias measured the distance and threw his hunting knife which stuck in the pig's ham and it turned and charged them. Humphrey couldn't move. It seemed the creature was running straight at him, foam flying from its jaws as it came. The two men with the deer started back along the trail, and the carcass fell off the pole. They left it and climbed the nearest tree.

Humphrey shut his eyes. He'd never see Eleanor's little baby . . . he hoped Georgie would look after Lion. . . . Then Manteo said "Faugh!" again, deep in his throat and the bow twanged and the arrow sped, straight to the heart of the racing animal. Humphrey sat down weakly. Mark Bennett called loudly for the skinners.

Dion Harvie made them all stop to rest and eat before going back. "We aren't used to this sort of thing," he said, firmly, "and I for one am still a little shaken. I hope I enjoy my piece of pork better than I expect to at the moment."

On the way home they took turns carrying the heavy burdens. It gave Humphrey his chance to tell Manteo about George Howe's last words and Towaye's presence at the pool. "Shall I tell the

Patentees what George said, Manteo? Do you think he knew something Simon did not tell the others? Is the colony in danger?"

Manteo said, "Wait! There is no danger while the navigator is still in the Sound. Wait until the feast is over."

"What has the feast to do with the threat of the Spanish?" Humphrey demanded.

"Let the Patentees have one thing at a time to think about. This feast is important."

"Do you mean that maybe everybody will like everybody else better when all the chiefs come to the feast?"

"You may hope so. The Governor hopes so. Those who come will leave with a good feeling. But not all will come. Towaye's tribe will not be there."

It was almost dark when they came out onto the knoll. Far away a dog howled. Lights flared on the beach and as the hunting party came closer, following the path from the chapel down to the houses, they could hear voices.

"Look, Manteo! What's going on? Something's wrong! They are calling Georgie."

Humphrey forgot the weariness and shock of the day in this new, unnamed fear and he was off, running, toward the lights.

CHAPTER 8

Towaye's Council Fire

As he approached, Humphrey could hear Eleanor calling, "Georgie, come back! I'm not cross any more. Come home and get your supper." Behind her Pastor Brooke was holding high a flaming pine knot. When she saw Humphrey she started to cry. "Georgie's lost, and it's all my fault."

She caught up her apron to wipe her hot face. It was smeared with soot from the torch and the tears had made streaks in the black.

"That goose! It hissed every time anyone but Georgie went near it, and it drove me wild. So I told him to go outdoors and tend it. And Lion followed . . ."

"Lion!"

"You didn't really expect anyone to look after him, did you?"

"When did you miss them? How long have they been gone?"

"We don't know. We've been searching since late afternoon. If he's off in the woods some- where, lost, he will be so scared. I hoped he had just gone to sleep down here on the beach. But he doesn't answer."

Eleanor's voice rose shrilly and 'Nias heard and came striding along.

"What's happened?" he asked.

The others who carried torches gathered round and the rest of the hunting party joined them. Manteo listened until the story had been told again.

"The little Georgie did not go far alone," he said, slowly.

"Then the puppy and the goose . . ."

"Were taken, too."

"Taken! What do you mean, Manteo?"

"You do not see in this another warning?"

The men had no choice then, except to tell the women about the arrows.

"Towaye!" Eleanor exclaimed. "How could he?"

The strained faces of the women and the stern ones of the men were easily seen in the light of the pine knots, each by the other.

"What shall we do? Standing here is no help."

Pastor Brooke said, "Manteo, will you take me to Towaye's village? Surely I can persuade him . . ."

"I will guide you," Manteo replied. "No one can put good in Towaye's heart. But if he has the child, we will bring him back."

"And Lion!" said Humphrey.

"You'd better come along and attend to that," said Pastor Brooke, smiling a little.

He lifted his hand to shield his eyes from the torchlight and looked at the crowd around him. "I'd like one other."

"I should like to be that one, Sir," said 'Nias. "Georgie is my . . . the same as our own child, now. I have the most right."

Pastor Brooke nodded. "I would say so, 'Nias. Yes, you should be the one."

The torches were used to light the others home. 'Nias saw Eleanor and the Widow Pierce safely on their way before he came back to the three waiting. Manteo led them to the spot where his canoe had been hauled up when he brought the fish earlier that day.

It was only a small boat, and Humphrey crouched between the knees of the two men who sat facing each other, while Manteo paddled at the stern. He was sheltered from the wind but had no mind for comfort. He tried to take deep breaths so his heart would not thump so hard. He was not afraid for his own safety. His fears were way out in front of the boat, imagining where Georgie might be now. He wished Lion had had time to grow into a larger dog if this had to happen. He might have saved Georgie. Saved? From what?

Humphrey remembered then the look on the young Indian's face one day aboard ship when he had stopped Georgie and measured the child's long locks with his hand. Though that hair had been cut long since, it wouldn't stop Towaye from taking . . . another . . . scalp. His own moved when he heard again the same mournful dog wail.

Opposite the big rock which Humphrey had marked on that other journey as being the neighborhood of Towaye's camp, Manteo brought the canoe round, said, "Now," and shot it through a wave, up the beach. When the water receded they stepped out and waited while he hid the boat. Then, speaking softly, Manteo gave directions.

"A path runs to Towaye's camp from this rock. We do not know what will be found there. I will go first and let the pastor follow me."

'Nias put Humphrey ahead of him and they started out single file. It was a well-used path. When the dog howled again it was much closer. Had it been coming from Towaye's village all evening?

Manteo stopped, said, "Wait!" and disappeared. The waiting seemed even longer than the walking. Would Eleanor be brave if they didn't find Georgie? They had to find him. Eleanor expected them to.

It was only then that Humphrey realized his own blame for everything. Eleanor had given him a home and asked for his help there. What help had he given? None of this would have happened if he had not gone hunting. Because he had wanted some fun he and these others were standing here late at night on a forest path and Georgie was probably crying somewhere, alone and afraid.

Humphrey felt his whole body burn with the shame of his guilt. He had thought he could be his own man in the New World. A real man took responsibility for things, as 'Nias was doing for his adopted son.

The next moment Manteo was there. He seemed, for him, a bit excited. "A strange thing has happened," he said. "You must see. I will take you, one by one, but the good pastor may say nothing to Towaye, now."

Had Manteo seen Georgie? Then Humphrey's mind was all on his feet, to lift them up and set them down, stepping without sound, his whole body concentrated on the act, until they reached the edge of the camp.

It was not a large one and it seemed deserted, Humphrey thought, though the smell of drying fish was everywhere. When his turn came, Manteo led him past some bark huts, pulled aside the branches of a bush and pushed him behind it. He heard a peculiar sound as the thick leaves settled round him and felt something rough against his face. He forgot the sound when a small line of light appeared at eye height and he realized he was looking inside a room through a crack in the wall of the cabin. When his eyes focused he almost exclaimed aloud in his surprise.

A council fire burned dully in the middle of the large hut. Around it, in order of dignity, sat the chiefs of Towaye's tribe. Towaye was there, looking sullen as always, and next him was Simon Ferdinando.

The navigator's lips were moving. He seemed to be speaking to the chiefs with Towaye's help as interpreter. Humphrey laid his ear to the crack, and almost exclaimed again. He hoped 'Nias and Pastor Brooke were near by and hearing, too.

Simon said, "The English are all alike, these and those others who burned your cornlands. And for what purpose? Because they want them for their own. They say there is room for all, but they will push you into the sea. Now, promise me to fight for Spain, and I will give you this . . ."

Humphrey strained to see what it could be. Something flashed in the firelight, and Simon held high the great silver goblet from the wall bracket in his cabin on *The Lion*.

"This is the cup," Simon went on, "which you were accused of stealing from the English admiral, Sir Richard Grenville. I will give it to you now, for your promise to help the Spanish King. Those I serve will not take your lands. They want gold. Keep the pearls you find in the little fish and the gold from the ground, for Spain. Do not let the English have it. They punished you wrongfully. Let your service to Spain be their punishment."

Oddly, Towaye did not look pleased. He spoke with his brethren and there was no agreement on the stolid faces.

Humphrey pressed harder against the thin wall and another lump of chinking fell out into the room. His breath almost stopped, but the

Indians were so intent that they did not notice. The hole was wider now and Humphrey could see farther into the room. By the entrance sat Tom the Lute and a sailor Humphrey did not remember. Tom had not brought his case. There was to be no music tonight. He seemed to be in all of Simon's evildoings. "I never want to hear Greensleeves again," Humphrey thought bitterly.

Simon turned the cup about to attract the Indians, but they shrugged and turned away. Towaye stood up.

"My brethren refuse the cup," he said, clearly. "We no trust any white man. It is a trick. You give the cup, then you come and search and say, 'Aha, they did take it that other time,' so we make no bargains now, about anything. This land is ours. The pearls are ours. The gold you may search for, but you will not find it." He pointed to the door. "Go, white man. We give you time. Go and tell the great Queen she may not make white camps here, and those others from Spain, they may not."

Simon Ferdinando did not trouble to hide his surprise. He tried to argue, but they held up their hands, palms out, and he was obliged to pack up the cup and leave, as Towaye urged.

Where was Georgie? Where was Manteo? He had a better chance now than he might, ever again, to get the cup. But he wouldn't take it, Humphrey knew. They had to find Georgie.

There was another reason why Manteo would not try to get the cup, tonight or any other time. The knowledge came to Humphrey slowly while he watched the Indians filing out of the Council House. Manteo had never said, in so many words, that he would get the cup. "If the Great Spirit wills." A white man had stolen it. A white man must restore it. Only so could Indian honor

be righted. Manteo had been waiting for him, Thomas Humphrey Hall, to see that. How dull he had been!

Humphrey moved a foot cautiously. It had gone to sleep, he had stood so still. Then he heard a familiar hiss, that odd sound he had not recognized when Manteo thrust him behind this bush. He moved his other foot and the hiss came again. He took a quick look into the hut. The fire was dying and all the Indians had gone. Where was Manteo?

Humphrey leaned over and felt quietly around his feet. He got a handful of soft feathers in his hand and a smart tap from Sir Walter's bill. If the goose was around, Georgie could not be far away. How long had the bird been there? He felt along the base of the hut and found Lion's soft muzzle. The puppy was sleeping and did not rouse when Humphrey whispered his name. He was curled in the shelter of Georgie's arm and the little boy was fast asleep, too. In the darkness Humphrey's hands went gently over the child. He seemed unhurt, but completely limp.

The bush moved. "Come now," Manteo whispered. "We will be safe."

Sir Walter hissed.

"Faugh!" said Manteo.

Humphrey said, "I will manage the animals. Somebody take Georgie."

He lifted the heavy bird, tucking him under his left arm, and got a good grip on the bill. Then he felt for Lion and Pastor Brooke whispered, "Never mind! I've got him," and then they were all making their way out of the sheltering bush and moving under the stars again, and Humphrey was struggling with the angry goose.

No one spoke until they were safely out on the water. Humphrey held Lion in the crook of his arm, and Sir Walter was hissing away like a kettle in the bottom of the boat and nobody caring.

The little dog had roused only enough to lick Humphrey's fingers and then he had gone soundly to sleep again.

"They must have been given something to make them sleep," said 'Nias anxiously, while he rubbed Georgie's hands.

Georgie said, "Don't, 'Nias, it hurts," and snuggled closer to him.

"Wake up, Georgie. Tell me what happened. What were you doing in Towaye's camp?" 'Nias shook the child, gently.

Georgie sat up, rubbed his eyes and yawned.

He sniffed the sea air, and looked up at the sky. "Where are we going now? I want to see Eleanor."

"You will, we are going home. Tell me what happened."

"Eleanor was cross at us, so I took Lion and Sir Walter down to the little beach where Humphrey washes me," said Georgie. "We went to sleep and when I woke up Towaye had come and he said he would give us a ride in his canoe. But he didn't give us any supper except some milk. Sir Walter didn't like it, but Lion and I were hungry. We drank a lot. And that's all. I'm so glad you came. Towaye's village smells. How did you find me?"

"It was Manteo," said Humphrey. "He knew the way to Towaye's village."

"But I was asleep," said Georgie. "I did not see him."

"Ah," said Manteo, "the women inside their huts were not asleep. They listened for something. I could feel it. The men were all in the Council House. Save one. He was on guard, but not by the entrance. What was he guarding? He had a dog and he let it howl. They will find them both when they go to look for their white hostage. That goose hissed at me. It told me why the dog howled. Then I knew why they had set a guard in that spot."

"They hadn't expected Simon, was that it, Manteo?" Humphrey asked.

"Yes, and they did not want him to see. So they made a mistake."

"And now we know the navigator for what he is," said 'Nias. "He's been suspected long enough."

"Shall we tell about the cup?" Humphrey asked, anxiously. What was he himself to do? Tell what he knew to complete the tale?

Before 'Nias could answer, Manteo said, "I pray you, my brothers, do not tell the chiefs at the meeting. Not yet. Show them first that some white men can be their friends. Wait!"

CHAPTER 9

A New Colonist

ELEANOR was still awake when they came in, and she hugged Georgie as if he had been gone a week. "Why do you cry?" he asked, wonderingly.

"Because I am happy you are found, and I'll never be cross again about that old goose."

At daybreak the story flew about the colony.

"I always said that Towaye was no good."

"But why did he do it?"

"The child was by himself and easy to take. He knows the ship is still here. He could have

bargained Georgie's safety against our returning to England."

"The Indians weren't using this part of the
island when we came. There is room for all of
us. Sounds dog in the manger to me," said Margery Harvie.

"Your cornfields weren't burned," said 'Nias.
"Whose were?"

"Towaye's. His tribe's, rather. While he was
in England. They say Sir Richard Grenville did
it because he thought they stole a silver cup of
his. It was very valuable old family silver."

"But we had nothing to do with it. Why hate
us?"

"How does he know we haven't cups to lose,
too?"

The Patentees held a meeting that night and
invited Manteo, Humphrey and Pastor Brooke
to attend. 'Nias had told Governor White the
rest of the story of Georgie's rescue.

"What can we do?" Roger Pratt asked. "He is
returning to England and could cut us off from
more supplies."

"Send him in irons to England."

"And who would navigate the ship for Captain Stafford?"

"You forget, gentlemen, that our tribunal sits

in England. We have no power here for such action," John White reminded them. "Simon knows that."

"Besides," said Dion Harvie, "what proof have we? Though we do have four eye-and-ear witnesses of his offer to Towaye, he did not tell how he got the cup. If we accused him, he could say that it was really Sir Richard who tricked the Indians. That the cup was given him in recognition of service. Such a thing couldn't be true, but we have no proof."

Humphrey fidgeted in his place. "Tell! Now is the time!" said his conscience. "These friends will protect you. Tell what you know, even though you, too, have no proof except Simon's own word."

His heart thumped wearily. Telling would not help. These men, though Patentees, could do nothing. They had said so. Simon would only laugh at them and deny everything. And he could still take him, Thomas Humphrey Hall, a minor, aboard *The Lion* to collect in England a rich reward from Uncle Jeremy. Nay, if he told, he himself would only be in greater danger. Simon would know it was he rather than one of those wretches from debtors' prison.

He looked at Manteo and the Indian's eyes

were on him. He shook his head slightly and
Humphrey knew then that Manteo had been
feeling his thought once more and was again
saying, "Wait!"

Ah! If Simon knew they knew, it would spoil
the chance of getting the cup back. Manteo
hoped that the honor of his blood brothers might
so be upheld. Towaye was right, Manteo was
white inside. He wanted only good for Towaye.
And possession of the cup would be a greater
thing than mere accusation of Simon.

Then Pastor Brooke spoke. "This is a difficult
thing for you," he said. "I am not a Patentee.
There will be no thought of prejudice if I prepare a letter to the tribunal, which Captain Stafford will carry for us when the ship sails. London
may then do as it likes with the wily adventurer.
Would that please you?"

It did please them. The pastor's plan would
take longer, that was all.

Humphrey fell asleep that night in the middle of a plan to get the cup off the ship.

From all the islands round, the Indians came
the next day, in ceremonial dress and with great
curiosity, aroused by the messages Manteo had
sent them, urging peaceful dealings with the

white man. Towaye and the other chiefs of his tribe were not there, but Humphrey was surprised to see the young prince who had helped Towaye spoil the pool, walking beside an older man who seemed the chief of all and was given great honor by the other Indians.

The warm air was heavy with a rich fragrance, the smell of freshly roasted meat. The whole colony had rallied to prepare the great feast which was held first. Pastor Brooke lifted his hands above them and asked for a blessing on all, impartially, food and partakers, before the serving began.

While the Patentees were meeting the night before, the Widow Pierce had superintended the construction of an outdoor hearth—a long, shallow trench with a frame above—where they roasted the deer, whole. All night men had worked there, turning it slowly above the bed of coals in the pit.

Manteo's mother came early that morning, and she had prepared the ducks which Mark Bennett supplied at dawn, according to his plan.

The greatest success was the pig. The Indians had accepted portions of everything quietly, except for grunts of satisfaction when a cracked marrow bone was presented to anyone. But when the pig appeared, that too, done crisply brown and whole, with a decoration of grapes covering its ugly mouth, loud exclamations of pleasure broke from the stolid group which told both cooks and hunters that their efforts had been worth-while.

The fort enclosure where the feast was spread was a litter of bones, torn bark plates, and melon skins and the guests' faces shone with grease in the mounting sun.

In the speech which Manteo made at the pow-wow following the eating, he strengthened his earlier urgings. He said: "There is room for us all on these islands and the mainland. These men know things that will help us. We know things that will help them. We must live as brothers. I have been in their land beyond the Great Water. I have seen their Queen. She did not order the punishment for the lost silver cup. Towaye's people must believe that. We must make them understand. Brothers in the family of the Great Spirit must not hate each other."

The young chief was sweating when he finished. But he was rewarded with guttural approval from his audience. The many speeches took a long time, as 'Nias had foreseen, because they all had to be interpreted, in both languages

When the chiefs went away, reluctantly, one party after another in their long, dug-out boats, and only Manteo and his mother were left, Pastor Brooke took them to the chapel. Manteo wanted to explain to his mother the white man's way of approaching the Great Spirit. Afterward the three stopped at the Dares's house to pay respects and found the Harvies with the assembled family and Henry Berry, talking over the day.

The Indian woman went at once to the fireplace to look at the strange utensils there, the three-legged cooking pots and the frying pans with the long handles so that a cook could stand well away from the heat. She had not had time in all the busy morning to see everything.

When they were ready to leave, she stood in front of her tall son and laid her hand on her bosom and said in English, "I, Mary."

"Oh, Manteo, we gave your mother an English name today. Her Indian one is too long for us," said Margery Harvie. "Do you mind?"

Mary was watching his face intently. His eyes gleamed like black coals in the dim room. "That is good," he said. "Today was good. You made a fine feast. Your guests felt they were welcome. Now you will be welcome here."

After the Indians had gone, Pastor Brooke said that Manteo's christening had been set for August thirteenth.

"It might seem a strange time," he added, "a weekday, Thursday and not even a saint's day, but Manteo's mother said it was an auspicious time by the moon for their tribe."

The christening itself was strange, Humphrey thought, as he later watched the ritual proceeding. Birds flew in and out of the open windows, chirping and twittering. There was no other choir. The candidate for baptism, though well dressed, wore deerskin clothes. His sponsor, Sir Walter Raleigh, was absent.

The pastor asked Manteo the questions and when he had given satisfactory response, John Brooke's voice grew even deeper as he said, "I baptize thee, Manteo, Lord of Roanoke and child of the Great Spirit, in the name of the Father . . ."

It seemed like Sunday. Humphrey had been excused from his Latin and the colonists had left their work to attend. People lingered near the chapel when they came out.

A great trimmed log lay beside Henry's ditch, ready to be hewn into useful lengths. Manteo stopped and measured it with his hands, critically.

"This would make a fine boat," he said. "If your carpenter people will come tomorrow to my village, I will teach the way. You have made a place for the Great Spirit and the fort is strong. You should now make boats."

He turned to Eleanor. "Will the White Doe allow the young Humphrey to go with us now? He may return with the others, tomorrow. There are many things he needs beside the Latin."

Humphrey looked anxiously at Eleanor, who

laughed and said, "You are right, Manteo. He may go."

There was the same wonderful confusion of dogs and children at Croatan. Manteo said, "Here you do not need the jacket," and Humphrey was glad to take it off. He wore his shirt of fine cambric until it clung to him in the heat of the boat-burning. When he removed that, too, the Indians stopped work and stared at his white skin. They did not laugh, but he felt ashamed. He appeared ill beside them.

"But I have a good muscle, Manteo," he said, flexing his arm. "I can work."

The log the tribe was fashioning was laid on cross supports on the beach. On top of it they had piled cedar gum, thickly, and set fire to it. When the layer of wood under it had burned away, they chipped out the burned part, shaping a little as they went, and repeated the process until the log was hollow enough for people to sit in. Then the thwarts for seats were fitted and they had a boat.

When Humphrey's back began to burn, Manteo sent him to sit in the shade of the huts with Mary. The fat she rubbed on him had a horrible smell but the feeling of relief was good.

Mary reached for his jacket and held it up
and shook her head, pointing from it to him and
then to the skins in her lap which she was fring-
ing. Somehow she made him understand that
one day she meant to make for him a suit of
clothes like Manteo's.

That would be wonderful. With loose, long
trousers like Manteo's he need not wear stockings at all. Eleanor had packed him three pairs
of knee stockings as the list had said and now
there was only one pair left whole in his chest.

In the twilight, when his shirt was dry and the
sun was gone, Mary led him about her garden.
Some of her cultivation had been made between
tree stumps. That was a new idea. He need not
wait to clear a space anywhere for his farm.
There was room enough behind their house to
start.

Early in the week following the carpenters'
boat lesson, when Humphrey went for his Latin,
his eyes were sparkling and he forgot the formal-
ity of greeting when he burst into Pastor
Brooke's study.

"The most wonderful thing! Mistress Dare
had a little girl, early this morning. She's not
much bigger than Lion."

"Splendid, Humphrey! We have too many

small boys. Have they given the little lass a name yet?"

"Yes," said Humphrey, chuckling. "She got it in sort of a funny way. It was Henry's idea."

"Henry's! What was he doing there?"

"He said the Widow Pierce needed some help on such a day. But that's my job, and he was mainly eating breakfast."

Pastor Brooke smiled. "Well, the Widow is an unusually good cook."

Humphrey said, "But it was a good thing Henry was there. 'Nias couldn't think of any girls' names. He wasn't prepared for a girl, it seems. He said name it 'Eleanor' and Eleanor said one of that name was enough. So, when Henry heard, he said why didn't they name her for her new country? Virginia. That did it."

The pastor nodded. "An excellent thought. Virginia Dare! It has a good sound."

"I wanted a Latin name," said Humphrey. "She's our first baby. Prima would have been better, I think."

"The other will please the Queen."

Humphrey was conjugating the verb "to serve" and wishing Lion would find his flea and sit still when Pastor Brooke interrupted.

"Do you know what day this is, Humphrey?"

"Tuesday," said Humphrey, promptly.

"No, no, boy, that is not what I mean. It's a significant day, Virginia Dare's birthday. You remarked that the little girl is the first child to be born in our colony. She is also, young man, as far as we know, the first white child to be born in the whole of the Queen's New World."

"So she may be," said Humphrey, cheerfully. "Perhaps you can say something about it at her christening, about hoping for lots more."

Overnight, following the birth of the new colonist, there seemed to be added duties for everybody in the Dare household. Humphrey chose to take over the morning errand for the milk. On the way he sat down on his favorite rock near the beach path, to think. It was easier, out of doors and alone.

The ship was there, out a little way in the Sound, sails shining in the morning sun. It had become as much a part of their scenery as the shore and woods. So far they hadn't found any gold for the navigator. What a mistake Simon and some other people had made about that!

He himself had had an idea that when a person reached the age of thirty he made no more mistakes. But look at the colony! Plenty of mistaken judgment had gone into its planning, as even he could see. Take the list of things each individual had been supposed to bring. "One pair of canvas sheets to make a bed. One rug to cover." Eleanor had brought all the blankets the Dares and Whites owned and a good thing, too. Manteo said it would be cold when the sea storms rose.

George Howe had brought only one suit for Georgie. They would have to cut down an old one of Humphrey's for him pretty soon. He had filled out like a young shoat the way the Widow Pierce stuffed him with food. The milk he drank!

Now that was another thing. Somehow he must make a deal, before anyone else thought of it, to buy the next heifer calf that came along in the Viccars' herd. He could have the start of a herd of his own before he got his farm, and they would have plenty of milk for both Georgie and Virginia.

Humphrey sighed. He had a lot to do, what with getting the cup from Simon, and planting a garden, and working up the business with Ambrose Viccars. His thoughts were interrupted by a shout from 'Nias.

"The milk, Humphrey! Mistress Pierce wants the milk."

CHAPTER 10

The Grenville Cup

THREE mornings later when Humphrey started after the milk he saw at once that *The Lion* was gone. Waves were crashing high on the beach and there was a strong wind, so that he had to struggle against it and some of the milk spilled. He felt a little sick, too. He hadn't recovered the cup and Pastor Brooke could not send his letter.

At home there was a little reassurance. A sailor had come with a message from Captain Stafford. The present storm, the letter ran, might last several days and the navigator thought it best

134

to stand out to sea to escape the pounding of the breakers. Meanwhile, his men were daily improving and when the storm blew off, *The Lion* was for England. Simon would bring her back into the Sound first, in case the colonists wished to return. Would they please lodge the messenger for the interval?

Humphrey was sent with the sailor to the men's bunkhouse and to call Pastor Brooke and when he came, he sat to breakfast with them. The wind was blowing harder now, and they could hear the fury of the waves even through the closed door.

The absence of the ship and the arrival of the message stirred the colony. Henry Berry came on the heels of the pastor and Dion Harvie arrived before the door was closed on Henry.

"The colonists want a meeting, Sir," said Dion.

"How can we hold one in this storm?" 'Nias asked.

"There's the chapel," said Pastor Brooke.

"Tomorrow, then," said Governor White. "People should take a little time to think over any plans they want to make."

"Excellent," said Dion, and the others agreed and everybody went away.

Humphrey could not keep his mind on his Latin that morning. Now he had to make definite plans to get the cup. He would need a small boat. If only Manteo would turn up with a fish or something! There was left one chance now, the night before *The Lion* sailed. His plans must be perfect. One chance!

Everybody went to the meeting next day except the Widow Pierce, Eleanor and the colony's children. The Patentees sat in front, facing the people.

Governor White said, "By this time you must all know the plans for *The Lion*. The Patentees are ready to listen to what you have to say."

Like a dam bursting, several were speaking at once. Governor White roared, above the wind, "One at a time, please."

"We have made a good beginning here. Let us stay, but make better plans."

"Our staple supplies are dangerously low."

"Someone should go to England and represent our situation to Sir Walter Raleigh. That person should remain there and be our agent for provisions."

"At least until we can reap our own husbandry."

"I'd like a plow."

"We should have brought more cows."

"The one who goes to England should be a good talker."

"Who would want to be that one, in any case? Just when we are getting started? I shouldn't."

"Send Governor White! Sir Walter Raleigh will listen to him."

Who had proposed the Governor? Humphrey could not distinguish the voice, and it was dark in the room because the shutters were closed. It had to be one of Simon's henchmen.

It was agreed, finally, that John White should be the one to speak for them in England, and his voice sounded pleased when he accepted the duty. How smoothly Simon's plans had been laid, Humphrey thought. But he had not meant the Governor to know as much of his activity as John White now did. They could yet have the last laugh.

Now Humphrey was plagued again by the old question. Should he tell the Governor about George Howe's warning?

As soon as Mistress Dare heard of her father's coming journey she sent Humphrey to fetch Pastor Brooke. They must arrange for the baby's christening, she said, the very next day.

The wind howled about the log house and the

sky was gray that August Sunday afternoon, the twenty-third, when Virginia Dare formally received her name.

For an altar, a small table was draped with a rich lace scarf of Eleanor's. It was set with pewter candlesticks, and Pastor Brooke brought his silver bowl that he had used for Manteo's baptism, ten days before.

The guests were the colony families and as many others as could crowd into the house. Manteo and his mother had come, in spite of the high wind, to see the new white child, without knowing about the ceremony.

When everything was ready the Widow Pierce came out of Eleanor's room, carrying the baby, and Eleanor and 'Nias followed her. Then Humphrey stepped forward to his place beside them, as Eleanor had directed him. He would be a very young godfather, and Pastor Brooke had hesitated a little in giving consent. But he was proud to be asked and he would keep his vows. He wore his best doublet, with the scarlet slashings and his last pair of whole stockings. Margery Harvie was to be godmother.

Pastor Brooke's surplice rustled a little against the pages of the Prayer Book. The air was stuffy on account of the closed door, but the booming of the sea was shut out and there was almost the same quiet in the log house as they usually had in the chapel.

"Dearly beloved . . ." the service began, and it went smoothly on to the part where John Brooke held out his arms and took the baby, sprinkling the little head with a few drops of the consecrated water. "I baptize thee Virginia Dare in the Name of the Father.. . ." and then the new Virginia's beginning whimper swelled to an angry roar. She was hungry.

Manteo and Mary had brought gifts for the baby, a string of miniature scalloped shells and a tiny birch-bark canoe, which measured the length of Humphrey's hand. It had been carefully made, even to the small paddle. Mary beamed when she sensed everyone's genuine admiration and said something in her own tongue.

"My mother says," Manteo explained gravely, "that the canoe is for good journeying for the fawn of the White Doe throughout her life."

Ananias bowed to Mary, from the waist. "Please tell her, Manteo," he said, "that the little girl's parents appreciate the good wish and the generous gifts."

When the service was over, Humphrey walked with Manteo to the beach. "I shall try to get the

cup the night before *The Lion* sails," he said, earnestly.

"Then the Great Spirit wills it to be. That is good. I have waited long."

"I know, and it's my only chance. I haven't tried before because Simon would have made trouble when he missed it. This way . . ."

Manteo nodded and finished, "Is a wise way."

"I won't be afraid, once I am on the ship. Getting out to it is the hardest part. The landing stairs won't be down . . ."

"I will bring a boat," Manteo promised. "You will get the cup."

They had three more days of bluster and roar before the wind died away to a stiff breeze. Doors and windows came open and the colonists emerged into the sunlight.

At midday *The Lion* was sighted beating in through the inlet, and Humphrey was sent with hurried messages, calling the Patentees and the pastor to a meeting at the Dares's house. There they would make plans for the governing of the colony in the Governor's absence.

Humphrey was not sent away when the men gathered, and he hunched himself very small down into a corner of the hearth to listen. When they had agreed to a division of responsibility among them, with Ananias nominally at the head, Dion Harvie spoke.

"There is one thing more, Sir. Suppose we are not here on your return?"

"Not here? Why wouldn't you be?"

"I mean Indians, Sir. If no one else has the courage to say it, I have."

"Now, now Harvie, don't get excited. Surely even Towaye sees that we are not to be scared away."

"I am not excited, Sir. But I have a wife, and

the safety of any two is involved in the safety of all. So let us be practical. There has been too little that was so, in planning this colony. Let us do something about a sorry business and plan a little, now."

"You are blunt, Harvie," said the Governor.

"It is necessary, Sir. I can't forget the silver cup. Primitive people nourish hates in the same way that some of us do friendship. Suppose Towaye starts a righteous war, a sort of protest against Manteo's change of religion. They know about it, no fear. He could hide a lot of his hate under such an appeal to the other tribes. What would save us, then?"

The Governor scowled. He said, "I think you are too apprehensive, Harvie. The only danger I foresee is the arrival of a Spanish ship. Spain is greedy for a foothold in the New World."

Humphrey sprang to his feet. The time had come. He must use his own judgment. Manteo was not here. "Sir, oh, Sir, please . . . George Howe said . . . I found him, you know . . . that we must beware of a Spanish ship. He seemed to know of a special one. Oh, Sir, you are right. One might come."

There was a shocked silence in the room. Humphrey expected a reprimand and it did not come. The Governor was pleased that his thought had been supported against Dion's!

"Howe was dying, Humphrey. He was no doubt delirious. I take little stock in what he said. But I do think, Harvie, that that is the greater danger."

Dion was scowling now, too. "It is fortunate, then, that we do have a small store of firearms and powder." His voice was bitter.

Roger Pratt, who rarely spoke, said, conciliatingly, "We need not name the danger, Sir. What we all want is an agreement of some kind, to give you information if we should not be here, when you return."

"You'll be here," said John White, stubbornly. He seemed to have forgotten completely, Grenville's unlucky fifteen and the earlier disappointed hundred who had sailed home with Drake.

"If we are not," Roger Pratt continued, as if he had not been interrupted, "look for a word of direction placed conspicuously."

"And the word?"

"If we go elsewhere, Manteo will be in it, in some way. Let it be a significant word, such as Manteo or Croatan or Mary."

"One word will not tell much. How will I

know if it has been a forcible departure or a chosen one?" the Governor asked.

Roger Pratt said, "If we choose to go, the word will be sufficient. If we do not, but go forcibly, we could agree on a sign to be added, I should think."

"You could use the cross," said John Brooke, softly. "It has stood for tribulation these centuries past."

"Let it be the word, then, gentlemen," said John White, rising, "and the cross, if necessary."

After supper that night Humphrey took Lion down to the big rock and waited there in sweating anxiety for dark to come. He'd have to take the puppy. He was a good excuse to get out of the house without question and he could stay in the boat with Manteo. Suppose Manteo did not come?

A boot scraped on gravel. The sailor messenger came along, carrying his duffel. He spoke to Humphrey carelessly and went on down to the beach. Presently one of *The Lion's* small boats could be seen approaching shore. Humphrey's heart skipped a beat. Maybe they'd let down the stairs for the sailor and he too could get up that way. If only Manteo would come!

Then Manteo said, at his shoulder, "Come. It is time."

He sent the light canoe shooting over the water and Lion curled up at their feet and went to sleep. There was no sign of the sailor or the other boat when they approached the ship. They circled it. The landing stairs were up. No hope there. Below the poop, something brushed against Humphrey's face and he reached and grasped the end of a thick, wet rope. Had the sailor gone up that way? It looked

as if he would have to, if he went at all. He must decide, now, because Manteo was having a hard time keeping the light canoe steady.

Humphrey tugged at the rope. It seemed fastened securely, above. The next moment he was clinging to it, with feet crossed and struggling up to the deck an inch at a time, like a fly going up a wall. Between frightened moments of wondering what would happen if he fell into the sea, he realized he hadn't thought of bringing anything to carry the cup in. He couldn't toss it down to Manteo in the dark. How would he get it away? His heart slowed and he chuckled, resting on the rope a moment. He hadn't got it yet!

Up and up. He was so high now he couldn't see Manteo. *The Lion* had not seemed so tall off Plymouth Hoe. And then his head was even with the railing, and he was over and hiding again in his old place behind the coaming. The ship was quiet. Once he heard a burst of laughter and the ghostly tune . . . Greensleeves. But Tom was not playing tonight. It was only in his head.

Then began one of the longest journeys Humphrey had yet attempted, slipping from shadow to shadow, hugging the railing and a protecting sail, looking around corners carefully and making slow headway until he stood outside Simon's door.

He tried the knob. The door was not locked. What if Simon were within? He couldn't hear any movement, but the door was thick, he remembered. He turned the knob and slowly released the catch until a crack of light appeared, but there was no roaring voice bidding him enter. Where was Simon?

Humphrey applied a cautious eye to the crack. The pointed black beard was slowly rising and falling in rhythmic beats on its wearer's chest. Simon was asleep, and across the room the goblet shone on its bracket in the guttering light of a night candle.

In two steps Humphrey stood under the bracket. In two more he was back at the door and the beard had not altered its motion. At the ship's rail he took off his jacket, ran a sleeve through one handle of the great cup, and tied the whole around his neck. Then he was overside and bumping down the rope to Manteo. The proof of the honor of his friend's blood brothers was in hand.

"Now Towaye must believe," said Humphrey, when he stood safely on land again.

"You must keep it hid then, until the Gov-

ernor has sailed," said Manteo. "He might want
to restore it to Sir Richard himself."

"Sir Richard would never see it, if it were
sent to him on that ship, right well you know,
Manteo," said Humphrey.

At the house the best hiding place was deep
at the head of the cradle under Virginia's mattress.

The whole colony left its work and flocked to
the beach the next day, the twenty-seventh, to
watch the Governor depart. The sand had been
pounded hard by the heavy waves. The sky was
free of storm clouds.

Governor White said, a little grandly, "I will
do my best to get the utmost for you, and I go
with the secure knowledge that I am leaving
you among loyal friends."

By sunset *The Lion* was out of sight. The
watchers had stayed on the beach until the last
tip of the highest sail caught a reflection from
the west and was gone. Then they walked back
up the slope to the clustered houses of the new
City of Raleigh, looking about them with a
clearer awareness of the place and their reason
for being in it. They were a colony of the Queen.

CHAPTER 11

My Lady Greensleeves

PASTOR BROOKE called the people together for a special evensong after *The Lion* had sailed, and nearly everybody went. Humphrey did not. He sat down on his rock and looked at the darkening sea for a long time. Church was all right. It made one feel better to kneel down and hear the firm voice of John Brooke reading the service, after Dion Harvie or 'Nias had done the lesson. But tonight he had to have more room to breathe, to sit still, to stop the pounding of his heart. *The Lion* had sailed and nothing had happened to him! The

149

navigator's threats had been empty, apparently, what the Widow Pierce called a case of green wood without a bellows. Now, except for the Latin, he was indeed a free man. And he had the Grenville cup!

Now he must do something about his farm. He would talk to Ambrose Viccars the next morning about that heifer calf. He still had his birthday florins. He couldn't think of a better use for one of them.

In the morning, on the way for the milk, he sniffed the air and found it soft and warm. He decided to slip down to the cove and have a swim. When he came round the bushes that screened it from the beach slope, Tom the Lute was there, grinning at him, the lute case slung over his shoulder. He was unshaven and his tattered clothes were stiff with salt.

"Tom!"

"I'm not a ghost, boy. Don't be scared!"

"But the ship's gone."

"Aye, and good riddance, too."

"Then you meant to stay."

"Aye, that I did."

Humphrey stared at the Welshman and the freedom he had felt the night before vanished and left his stomach in a hard knot. Simon was laughing somewhere out there on the sea. He had left a watchman behind. There was no other possible reason for Tom to be here.

Tom returned Humphrey's suspicious look with a wide grin. "Your friend Simon was in a rare taking yesterday. At the last minute he missed something valuable . . . He had the ship searched. When he misses me, too, he will think . . . what he will think."

He took out his lute and strummed a chord. "Simon was a man bearin' watchin', Master Humphrey, an' I bore it, until the need was gone. That's the Almighty's truth. I came only for this." He strummed again and sang softly, "And who but Lady Greensleeves?"

Humphrey told himself stoutly not to be fooled. Simon had only pretended to sail. He had set Tom ashore as a decoy, and he would bring the ship back in after dark and take them both aboard. Because there had been no gold here the navigator meant to collect a handsome reward from Uncle Jeremy. Humphrey's mouth felt dry and his knees began to shake. He would not go without a fight.

A pebble rolled at his feet and another. Tom had his finger at his lip and was making silly faces. Was the man crazy, too? And where had he slept the night, if he had come ashore when the ship sailed?

More pebbles came rolling down and a voice said, "Oh, Tom, you did manage! I've been frantic," and there was Margaret Lawrence, spinster, standing among the bushes above the cove.

Humphrey looked from one face to the other and then his heart eased. This was love. He grinned weakly at Tom. The lady, walking on the beach on their first night here. The lady, crying because the sailors were ill. Before that, the lady having lute music for children's games on the ship. Tom's Lady Greensleeves.

Margaret tried to jump back when she saw Humphrey, but all she did was turn her foot, grasping at a bush which came out by the roots. Then she was rolling down onto the sand. Tom and Humphrey jumped to try to catch her and collided and the three landed in a heap, with the lady's skirts trailing in the water.

When Margaret, sputtering and spitting, had the sand out of her mouth, she said, "Humphrey Hall, you go fetch Pastor Brooke here. Quickly, now."

"Stop, boy!" said Tom, though Humphrey hadn't stirred. He turned to Margaret.

"Are ye then daft, woman, to think of having

a marryin' on the beach? There's you, looking as ye are, with sand in your hair and your kirtle wet. And my decent suit still in the chest ye brought ashore for me. There's also the banns. The pastor would be first to remind ye of them, after me."

"But Tom, there's no place for you, else." She looked ready to cry.

Tom and his Margaret had been most decorous, Humphrey thought. Not even the Widow Pierce had suspected their plans. He said, slowly, "There's Governor White's room. At our house."

"Humphrey! So there is! But do you think Mistress Dare would offer?"

"She might, if she knew about Tom."

Margaret threw her bush away and held out a hand to each. "Let's go tell her," she said.

Eleanor exclaimed, shrilly, when she saw them, "The chanteyman! But we saw *The Lion* go out to sea yestere'en."

Tom nodded. "Yes, ma'am, and I was under the beach bushes, waiting for daylight. I'm not really fitten to come in, Mistress Dare, but I'd like . . ."

Then Margaret Lawrence found her tongue. "I . . . we . . . he . . . Oh, Mistress Dare, he has come to be a-marrying with me, and can he stay here until the banns be read?"

It was a long, exciting day. That evening, while the fire crackled on the hearth because the sea chill was on, Humphrey studied how to approach the Widow Pierce with his latest problems. He and she were alone, except for the baby, asleep in her cradle.

"I've just thought of something, Mistress Jane," he began. "All the children in this colony are boys. If I have my farm, I'll have to find me a wife, someday. And there won't be anybody for me."

"I'm the one to be doing that kind of worry-ing," she retorted, clicking her knitting needles furiously. "Plenty of time for you. And when it comes you won't have to look far. Not farther'n your foot, might say."

Humphrey looked at his foot. It was almost touching the cradle. A little effort, and he could give it a push and Virginia would oblige with a nice, loud yell. It was fun, sometimes, to watch the angry beating of her tiny fists. She didn't like to be rocked for some reason. Perhaps he ought to put the cup somewhere else, he thought, uneasily. But surely she couldn't feel it through the thick mattress. He'd have to tell, sometime, of course.

He stretched his foot a little farther, eyeing the Widow.

"Now, now, none of that, Master Humphrey. Not when I've just got her off. Wait until she's the right size to tease, the way 'Nias does Elea-nor."

"Then you mean we'd be marrying, same as they?"

"For a boy that studies Latin, Humphrey Hall, you're kind of dull, 'times."

"It's this farm on my mind, Mistress Jane. I got me a heifer calf today."

"You don't say! Where you planning to keep it?"

"Well, Mark Bennett says he can make me a lean-to."

"Leaning on what?"

"This house. The mother died, birthing it, and I've got to raise it. I thought maybe you'd help. Ambrose Viccars let me have it for nothing, though I offered to pay."

"Then he thinks it will die. We won't let it." The knitting dropped in the Widow's lap. "Humphrey Hall, what have I said? We! I'm a good mind to listen to that Henry Berry. Marryin' with him would be peaceful, compared. First, here, it's that big-eyed Georgie that a body can't no ways fill up. Next a pup-dog learning to live in a house with a dirt floor. Then Miss Virginia arrives with her notions about not bein' rocked. 's what a cradle's for. Comes today that chanteyman for a boarder for three weeks, singin' for every meal, not just supper. And *you* want me to help raise a heifer by hand."

The Widow stopped for breath and Humphrey studied his foot. About a quarter-inch more would do it.

"Master Humphrey, you leave that cradle be and get at your lesson."

Instead, Humphrey went out into the twilight and Lion trotted after him. He followed
now, without invitation. He was getting too
heavy to carry. The calf looked the same as when
Humphrey had last seen her, an hour before.
He hung over her in the Viccars' byre, seeing
every hair and line. She was a plain brown bossy
except for the white patch on one rump and the
white forehead. He meant to have a large herd
and the names would all be Latin. This one was
the first, so she must be Prima. He was glad they
had not used it for the baby. Prima, Hall's Pride.

Henry Berry was just leaving when Humphrey arrived back on the home doorstep. He
said, "Master Humphrey, I hear you've started
your livestock."

"An orphan calf is all."

"I wanted to make certain," said Henry. "It
does seem kinda strange to mix up a heifer calf
with a marryin'."

"What do you mean, Henry?"

"I've got the Widow's consent tonight, condi-
tional-like. She won't consider me putting up a
new house. Says I can go my way and she'll go
hers, less'n I move in here. Since Providence has
sent her another critter to look after, she can't
see it any other way."

"Mark is going to build me a little shed. I asked her would she help me feed the calf. Takes two, sometimes, first off."

Henry said, "You know what I think? The Widow Pierce is all mixed up. The calf is only a good reason. It's that baby. It wouldn't be raised right if she left now."

"We'd hate to see her go, too, Henry. When will you publish the banns?"

"This coming Sabbath, if the pastor agrees. He already has Tom the Lute's."

"Try for a double wedding," said Humphrey, "and we'll invite all the Indians and have another feast."

By mid-September the banns had been published the required three times and the double wedding was held in the following week, but only Manteo and Mary were invited, outside the colony.

It was a mellow day, warm and still. The contented hush in the chapel when Pastor Brooke began the marriage service matched the weather.

There was only a little finery. The Widow Pierce had said, when clothes were mentioned, "Nonsense. I'll stand up in my best linsey-wool-sey, which Henry has seen before, and he can take me that way or not at all."

Margaret had been delighted when Eleanor offered, for a veil, the lace scarf which had adorned Virginia's christening altar. It went beautifully with the pale folds and puffs of an English taffeta which Margaret had never unpacked.

Getting married was a completely worthwhile process, Humphrey decided, later, as he followed the wedding party home. They were to drink the brides' health at the Dares's. It would only be a new kind of tea, made from sassafras bark, but the toast part at least would be like old England.

Toasts! Why not drink them from the Grenville cup? Producing it now would be a little different from flatly announcing to the Patentees that he had got it away from Simon.

The main room was crowded, but the day allowed overflow outdoors. The table was covered with a fair cloth today and the steaming punch was carried in by 'Nias. Eleanor was about to fill the mugs each person had brought when Humphrey said, "Wait!"

He stepped to the cradle and felt beneath the mattress, and drew out the great cup, holding it as high as he could. "Only this is fit for a wedding toast," he said.

A babel rose.

"The lost cup!"

"Is it really the Grenville? Then it isn't lost."

"Now Towaye will sing another tune."

"Where did you get it, Humphrey?"

"I stole it!"

"But how could you?"

His story reduced the brides' importance a little while it lasted, and then the babel broke out again, as the goblet, somewhat tarnished, but still serviceable, flew from hand to hand.

"Simon Ferdinando! Imagine!"

Dion Harvie shook Pastor Brooke's hand. "That letter idea of yours was splendid, Sir, though I wish the boy had acted sooner."

"But you see, he had threatened me, too," said Humphrey, hearing. "I was too scared to tell anybody but Manteo."

"You weren't too scared to go and get the cup," said Pastor Brooke.

"I had to do that, Sir," said Humphrey, feeling his face growing red at the praise.

The cup added zest to the wedding supper, too, one more feast before they settled in earnest making the colony snug for cold weather. Manteo had warned of winter storms and showed them how to pack leaves which the children gathered, against the foundations of the houses. Logs were rechinked, inside and out.

Nuts were ripening in the woods, and on a golden afternoon in early October, Tom and Henry Berry and Dion Harvie made up a party with 'Nias, to supply their several houses with walnuts. At the last minute they said Humphrey could go if he would leave Lion at home. The men were making for a patch of woods about a mile beyond the fort, where the yield had been reported unusually thick.

Humphrey found a full-bearing tree and began picking up those already fallen among the leaves. He was dreamily planning a walnut plantation on his farm when he heard a rustling on the other side of the thicket. One of the party, he thought, comfortably, or it might be a deer.

The bushes parted the next moment, and he looked full into the face of Towaye. Only then he realized how still the woods were. The others must have moved way ahead. He felt a prickling of apprehension up his back, but said, steadily, "Oh, Towaye, you have heard surely about the cup? We have it now and shall send it back to its owner. Then all the world will know that your tribe did not take it. Won't you be friends?"

"All the Indians know," said Towaye, "but that man is gone. You are here. Nothing is changed. One white man or another white man, always he takes. Never does he give. We will push you into the sea."

"We want to give you our friendship, to teach you. Surely that is giving."

"But you take our food," said Towaye, contemptuously. "These nuts. These are my woods. Friendship! Faugh!" The bushes were pushed together again as if a door had been shut in Humphrey's face.

He leaned to pick up his basket. He wanted to tell 'Nias quickly. He heard a small "ping," turned, and received an arrow full in his chest. The force of it knocked him over, and though he was afraid he couldn't make a sound, he was so scared he shouted with all the breath left him for 'Nias.

When 'Nias came he touched the arrow gently and it came away easily in his hand. There was no blood, only a tear in Humphrey's jacket. 'Nias felt inside.

"Thank God!" he said. "It hit your ring. A real lucky piece, Humphrey."

The others came panting after, with partially full baskets.

"I saw Towaye," Humphrey told them, excitedly, sitting up, "and we talked and then he went away and out of the air this arrow came, right at me."

"But there's no blood," said Henry. "Didn't it hurt you?"

"Show them the reason," said 'Nias.

They walked carefully on the way home, conscious now of every bush or unusual sound.

Towaye's latest arrow changed the face of things, a little, that winter. Not all of Manteo's people went to the mainland, as was their custom. A few remained in the bark huts on Croatan Island, among them Manteo's family.

"That does make me feel better," said Margery Harvie, when she heard of it. "I don't dread the cold as much, now, somehow."

Building went on, inside the fort, until men's hands grew too cold and stiff to hold their tools. The days grew shorter and the weather colder.

When contrary winds drew the heat up the chimneys and the houses were cold at midday, more than one colonist questioned their wisdom in remaining. Perhaps the women and children should have returned to England with *The Lion*. Not even Christmas, with deer meat on every spit, could quite overcome those doubts.

Humphrey could not forget the naked hate in Towaye's eyes and voice. Would the Indian boy never stop until he had driven the colonists away? If a Spanish ship should come, how would Towaye fight two enemies at once? Which one would he join to rid himself of the other? Would he side with Spain long enough to destroy the City of Raleigh?

These questions threaded through all Humphrey's plans for garden and farm and manor, and he knew that he was waiting for something. What would Towaye do next?

CHAPTER 12

Battle for Roanoke

IT grew bitterly cold after Christmas. Outdoor work became only a matter of cutting enough wood to keep reasonably warm. One night Humphrey was wakened by the thrust of Lion's cold nose against his cheek. "Down, boy! It isn't morning yet."

But Lion wouldn't down. He walked to the door and scratched on it, whining a little before he came back to the bed.

Humphrey said again, "Down, boy. Go to sleep!" But Lion only pawed at the covers and returned to the door.

165

His master groaned. "Lion, it's too cold . . .
Oh well . . ." He threw back the blankets and
dressed hastily, his teeth chattering. Before opening the house door he grasped Lion's collar, safe-
guarding a possible dash after deer scent. Lion
was no longer a puppy. He marched abroad as
high as Humphrey's knee nowadays.

Earlier in the evening there had been a thick
fog. Now it was lifting a little and hung like a
gauzy curtain between the houses and the rising
moon. Lion strained at the collar, leading the
way straight up the hill toward the fort.

Out in the fresh, keen air, Humphrey was
wider awake. He pulled Lion up short and stood
a moment in the path, listening. There was no
unusual sound, nothing but the waves on the
beach, dulled a little by the mist.

The next second the dog had bolted, barking
furiously. Humphrey stood a moment longer,
undecided what to do. Perhaps he ought to go
back and get Henry and his gun. He might better see what the trouble was, first. Now it seemed
there were two dogs barking. Propelled by sud-
den fear, Humphrey ran, the blood from his
pounding heart roaring in his ears. Lion was the
only dog in the colony.

There were two dogs, he saw, when he came

out onto the leveled space in front of the fort. The stranger was larger and darker than Lion. They were snarling and yapping, feinting and retreating, and as Humphrey watched, they clinched and rolled over and over, each trying for the throat-grip that would end the battle.

Lion was getting the worst of it. Humphrey circled, hoping to help him. But the two dogs were wound together as one and impossible to separate. The smell of fresh blood rose, mixed with the strong, salt smell from the sea.

Humphrey screamed, "Lion!"

"Yah!"

Something flashed from the fort gateway in the growing moonlight. Towaye stood there and held a knife, poised, ready to throw.

"I kill your dog," he exulted. "You shall not have. Manteo should not give you."

He raised his arm. Humphrey screamed again and jumped. The knife was knocked out of Towaye's hand, and he off his feet by the impact of Humphrey's body against him. When they fell, Towaye was on top and clawing.

Blood ran into Humphrey's eyes and he couldn't see, but he got one hand free and into Towaye's stomach. Then they, too, were rolling as one, over and over on the frozen ground and no holds barred. They collided with the dogs, once, and Humphrey smelled their hot breath. There was a sharper yelp. Was it Lion? Humphrey shook the blood away so he could see.

Towaye's dog was making for the woods on three legs and Lion lay still. It was too much. With a mighty heave, Humphrey slammed Towaye over, flat on the ground and sat on him. He grasped the Indian's straight hair in both hands and held his head still, so, and did not hear hard boot-thumps on the hill path.

"Listen to me, Towaye," he gasped. "You're a stupid Indian. Fighting when we all could be friends." He banged Towaye's head on the ground a couple of times for emphasis. "When I let you up, you follow your dog. Mine has beaten him in fair fight. Don't you come back here until you are willing to be our friend." He thumped Towaye again.

Towaye's breath was short, too, from being sat on. He blurted, "Indian . . . takes prisoner . . . in fight . . . or kills."

"But I couldn't kill you, Towaye, and you wouldn't like being a prisoner."

"Towaye die first."

"Well, it's not going to be either one, but if my dog is dead, I'll fight you again."

He got up wearily, turning to Lion and did not see Towaye leap for the fallen knife.

'Nias' voice boomed out of the mist. "Drop it, Towaye, and follow your dog."

Towaye spat and was gone.

Lion whined when Humphrey touched him.

'Nias said, "You young fool! He could have killed you."

Henry Berry arrived then, breathless and half dressed and shivering. "What's going on? Yelling around and scaring the women half to death!"

Then he saw Humphrey working over Lion and at 'Nias' nod, looked at the bloody battle-ground. 'Nias explained what he knew.

"Lion's going to be all right," said Humphrey, standing up. "Got the breath knocked out of him, is all, and a few cuts. Good old boy! Sent that cur packing, didn't you?"

"How'd it happen? What's Towaye want, dead of night? No good, I vum."

"He was in the fort," said Humphrey.

They went inside and looked around. He had left his flint. It was lying near the first of several small bundles of fine-shredded bark, dry pine cones and fluffy old grass, evenly spaced against the stockade, all of it stuff that would catch quickly. Towaye had come to burn the fort.

After that, the night watch they had only talked about before began its vigil, the men of the colony in pairs in turn, and the winter wore on. There were other petty annoyances, but none as terrifying as Towaye's attempt.

"We don't scare easy," Henry Berry said again, when one of the Viccars' cows was found hamstrung and had to be killed.

When spring came, Humphrey started a garden between the tree stumps behind the house and Mary herself came to show him how to plant corn, with a fish head in each hill to give the roots greater nourishment. She showed him, too, how to fence his bit of land with thick brush, tied together with strong leather strings she supplied, to keep the deer out when the corn shoots appeared.

Beneath the renewed daily activity outdoors there was a growing uneasiness throughout the colony, which everybody felt and nobody mentioned. Humphrey wondered if it was because the ship did not return. Or Towaye? What could he do, now that they kept a guard?

The odor from the heifer's lean-to drifted in the open windows when the days grew warm and 'Nias shook his head at Humphrey one day at table. He said, solemnly, "If you don't get that farm pretty soon, to keep all this livestock on, young man, the Mistress Dare and I may be obliged to present you with this place for your manor house and we'll go elsewhere."

Humphrey was looking down, sharing a bite with Lion, and did not see 'Nias wink at his wife. He asked earnestly, "But where would you go?"

"A bull's-eye for you," said 'Nias. "The point is, where?"

There was still no sign of the returning ship,

and the grapes had begun to ripen again along the beaches when Humphrey took Eleanor his first crop of maize. They sat admiring the basketful of tiny ears.

"I'm a real farmer now, Eleanor. I wish . . ."

"Yes, Humphrey? You should finish, once begun."

"I'd like Uncle Jeremy to see my crop."

"You're a forgiving person, Humphrey Hall! When he practically drove you away from home."

"Yes, but he drove me to this. The only thing I couldn't forgive would be if he was mean to Tobey."

She shook her head. "He wasn't."

"You don't really know that."

"Ah, but I do. I have never found the way to tell you."

Humphrey stood up. "You mean he's dead?"

Eleanor nodded. "The day after you left. Old Robin thinks he knew you weren't coming back. When they untied him he went up to his mat by your bed and he never got up again."

"Thanks," said Humphrey, gruffly, and rushed outdoors.

He sat on his rock and looked at the water a long time, not seeing it. "If only I could have brought him!" he mourned. "He might have lived, here."

He heard a footstep and smelled the odor of somebody's bad breath, very close. A low voice said, "Master Humphrey, might I speak with ye, a minute?" It was one of the cowed debtors he had seen in Simon's cabin.

"There's talk, goin' round, Master Humphrey."

"About what?"

"Gettin' away from this place, like. Governor White not returning and all, some are kinda fidgety. They say the place ain't safe, any more. I just wanted to urge ye, Master Humphrey, now that they're lettin' ye vote, to have a mind to one thing if it comes up. Movin', I mean. 'Twould be good for yerself to get away, too. So Simon can't find us, that is. Ye see how 'tis, boy."

Humphrey said, "I see how it is for you. Go if you like, whatever the rest of the colonists do. I, for one, will vote to stay here. The Indians must not think they are strong enough to drive us away. We came to make this our home."

"But Master Humphrey . . ."

"I said I would vote to stay," said Humphrey, firmly.

On returning to the house, he said cheerfully,

"Another month and Virginia will be a year old."

"Yes," said Eleanor, "and what future has my child? She will be no more than an Indian squaw by the time she is my age. Look at me!" She thrust a foot at Humphrey. "Do you see any difference between me and Mary this minute? Deerskin shoes. My hair in braids because my snoods are torn and past mending. I get so tired of being brave, Humphrey."

Everyone had a different worry, he thought. Manteo had a new one in late July when he appeared one day and asked for 'Nias.

"The old chief is dead," said Manteo. "The one who has held all of the tribes together, more than I. Some of them will break away now. His son is Towaye's friend."

Humphrey thought of the tall boy who had come to the feast. It must be he. Would he be chief in his father's place?

'Nias asked Manteo to wait while he called the Patentees together.

"Towaye hasn't been idle," said Dion Harvie.

Manteo nodded. "He preaches one sermon and every day more of my brethren are believing him. He says the white man must be driven into the sea."

"If only the ship would come!"

"What good would that do? Stop Towaye?"

"No, it's the supplies, man. We need those for a successful siege."

"Siege!"

"You heard Manteo. It could come to that."

That was the day it first occurred to Humphrey that it might be a good idea to learn how to shoot an arrow from a bow. They had all been stupid, not to learn. It was useful knowledge which they might need. He asked Manteo for lessons.

Whether it was Simon's frightened henchman or Eleanor's annoyance about her clothes, Humphrey could not afterward decide. But he, too, became more conscious of the anxious waiting for John White to return. He took to climbing every morning to a high spot above his cove to watch for the ship, without telling anyone. Sometimes Georgie and always Lion went with him.

Hidden by the high grass at their backs and with the sea at their feet, far below, it was a pleasant way to spend an hour or two, and discouraging to go home afterward without having seen the sign of a sail.

One morning when Georgie had not come,

Lion cocked an ear and began his deep growl, and Humphrey silenced him just in time. To-waye's head appeared on a ledge below, where he too sat for a long time, looking out to sea. What was he watching for? Did he know he was not alone?

Then a day came when the waiting was over. Georgie sat weaving a small grass basket, taught him by Mary, and Lion lay panting near. The air was heavy, as if a storm might be blowing up. Humphrey had his Latin book, but he was not studying. This self-appointed watching was a waste of time, he thought, when he might be working in his garden. He threw the book down and rolled over on his stomach, looking at the sea, with his chin propped on his hands.

There was movement in the haze above the water, and his eyes focused sharply out of their dreaming, and he saw a ship, standing in toward the inlet. It was not *The Lion*. This one's lines were lower and more clumsy. Surely it was not an enemy . . . His heart raced.

But he forced his voice to be steady, when he spoke to the child. "Georgie, do you remember the secret you had with your father? The time he told you to run fast and hide if you saw a Spanish ship?"

Georgie dropped the basket. "I remember. But it never came."

"I think it has, now," said Humphrey. "Look!"

He held Georgie's hand while they watched it together, and as it came nearer the unmistakable yellow and red emblem of Spain broke out at her mast.

"The time has come for you to run, Georgie. But Lion will go with you. Run to the fort. That's the best place to hide. Tell Henry why you have come. It isn't a secret any longer, Georgie. It is all right to tell. Run, now! I'll come just behind you."

Georgie thrust his arm through Lion's collar and they set off down the path to the cove. Humphrey waited to see if there was movement on Towaye's ledge. The whole colony could reach the fort by the time the Spanish ship anchored in the Sound unless Towaye's tribe chose that good moment to appear. . . . He set his teeth. He would not let himself think of that.

Then he, too, was running, by a difficult short cut, which would bring him out below the houses so that he could warn the women.

Georgie must have run like a deer. The hill was alive with movement when Humphrey reached home. He met Eleanor and Mistress Berry carrying the cradle between them. It was piled high with odds and ends of need, and only Virginia's head was visible.

"The cup!" said Humphrey. He dashed back for it and seized his bow and quiver of arrows.

"We'll give an account of ourselves," said Henry Berry, when Humphrey appeared. "That little Georgie didn't turn a hair. Said his piece like a soldier, he did."

Even though they had been half preparing in their minds for what was happening, the confusion inside the fort was worse than any dock, until Dion Harvie issued stern orders. "We may be in here a week, or a month, or we may all be dead tomorrow. The first thing is food, and the second thing is dressings for wounds."

"Oh, I left my herbs behind," the Widow Pierce lamented. There was a chorus of other afterthoughts. 'Nias headed a detail to go and collect. After that the fort gate was shut.

The first shower of Indian arrows hit the stockade that afternoon, along with the first boom of the *Santa Lauria's* guns. The City of Raleigh was in state of siege. Towaye had joined fortunes with the stranger to drive out the Englishmen.

Few slept the first night. Again and again the Indians attempted to set fire to the stockade. Humphrey was told off to stand a watch. He did not feel tired or excited . . . he couldn't feel anything, he was sure, except the dull ache deep inside of him because Manteo was not there with them. Would Towaye's people turn on him, too?

When Henry's deep ditch prevented firing the stockade, the Indians began shooting flaming arrows inside. Terror mounted, then, as the full meaning of their situation became clear to the women. The children screamed and the defiant yells of the Indians grew louder with each shot from a colonist's gun. Dion had counseled careful aim to make each one count.

It was perhaps three in the morning when the ground shook under their feet and they heard a distant boom.

"What was that?"

The next instant the whole sky was lighted by a great sweep of flame.

"The houses! Our houses are burning. The Spanish guns have got the range!"

"No," said Humphrey, looking through his sentry loophole recklessly. "Not the houses. It's farther away. Oh, it's the ship! It's burning, all over."

They listened. They could hear nothing now but the roar of the flames, and gradually the odor of charred wood drifted up the hill on the dawn wind.

Humphrey's watch ended, and he stepped down from the parapet. 'Nias took his place. "You can take a nap," Humphrey said. "The Indians have stopped shooting. Maybe the ship blowing up frightened them off."

"That's the time not to take a nap," said 'Nias. "It's a way they have. They'll be swarming back again, when they think we don't expect them."

But when morning came the colonists were still undisturbed. It was strange. Humphrey looked out. In front of the fort gate, in almost the spot where the dog fight had occurred that long past winter night, lay one still body, on its side, the face half turned toward the watchers from within.

"It's Towaye," said Humphrey, in an awed voice. "Let's bring him in here. If he's hurt, maybe Mistress Berry can help him. And he'd be the best prisoner we could take."

"It could be a trick, too," said Henry, "to get us out there. We'll wait a while."

When an hour dragged by and nothing had happened, Humphrey insisted that they open the gate. The scornful Towaye would not lie that long, even for the sake of a trick.

They opened the gate cautiously. Towaye was dead from a colonist's gun, though he looked only asleep, as he might have been before he had learned to hate.

"I think the battle's won," said 'Nias slowly. "He was a strong leader and without him they fell apart."

There was movement in the path toward the beach. It was Manteo, and another Indian, younger and hesitant, was with him.

"It's Towaye's friend, the chief's son," said Humphrey.

"The Spaniards will not trouble you," said

Manteo. "Their boat exploded and they died of it."

"Did you help that explosion a little, Manteo?" 'Nias asked.

The gleam was there, far back in Manteo's eyes, Humphrey saw. "They were my enemies, too," he said.

The young chief had knelt beside Towaye's body. Now he stood, looked at Manteo, as if for reassurance, and turned to Humphrey. He spoke in faltering English.

"You, brave boy. I, friend." He looked down at Towaye. "He teach me, but I . . . no hate . . ." He could not finish.

ROANOKE
ISLAND

ATL

OC

ML